GARRY DISHER

PAYDIRT

WYATT · BOOK TWO

untapped

ABOUT *UNTAPPED*

Most Australian books ever written have fallen out of print and become unavailable for purchase or loan from libraries. This includes important local and national histories, biographies and memoirs, beloved children's titles, and even winners of glittering literary prizes such as the Miles Franklin Literary Award.

Supported by funding from state and territory libraries, philanthropists and the Australian Research Council, *Untapped* is identifying Australia's culturally important lost books, digitising them, and promoting them to new generations of readers. As well as providing access to lost books and a new source of revenue for their writers, the *Untapped* collaboration is supporting new research into the economic value of authors' reversion rights and book promotion by libraries, and the relationship between library lending and digital book sales. The results will feed into public policy discussions about how we can better support Australian authors, readers and culture.

See untapped.org.au for more information, including a full list of project partners and rediscovered books.

Readers are reminded that these books are products of their time. Some may contain language or reflect views that might now be found offensive or inappropriate.

ONE

The work was dirty, the little town a joke, but Wyatt was interested only in the advantages—they didn't know who he was, there were no cops, and no one was expecting a payroll snatch.

He was up to his elbows in grease when the money arrived. The Steelgard security van appeared at the cemetery corner in a cloud of dust, crept past the bowling green clubhouse, and slowed for the gate in the temporary fence that separated the construction camp from the town. He watched the van lurch through the gate into the camp and stop outside Brava Construction's site office, fifty metres from where he was getting his hands dirty. He checked the time: midday. He saw two men get out. They began to haul cashboxes into the site office. When one of them glanced in his direction, Wyatt bent over his work again and got some more dirt on himself.

He was in the Brava Construction repair shop, servicing gearboxes. On previous Thursdays he'd been with the crews laying pipes across the wheat flats north of the town, but this time he'd paid one of the Chileans fifty bucks to swap with him and now he was up to his elbows in grease, watching the money arrive.

Normally Wyatt never pulled a job from the inside. If he was in a city he'd base himself in some distant suburb and strike out of nowhere. But this wasn't a city, this was Belcowie, population two hundred, a dusty farming town three hours' drive north of Adelaide. It had a Four Square store, a post office, four massive grain silos, a garage with a solitary petrol pump, a bank open two afternoons a week, fifty houses, no police station, and a long, low pub that had never had it so good.

Brava Construction had hired one hundred and fifty men

when it got the contract to lay the gas pipeline. All of them had a big thirst. Oddly, a third of them came from South and Central America. The boss was an Argentinian called Jorge Figueras, and he'd tell anyone who listened that it was his duty to help others who'd fled from poverty, death squads, generals and communists. It was a ten-month contract so the wages were high. One hundred and fifty men at $1500 a week, a further $50 000 in managers' wages and expenses—$275 000. But the Steelgard van also did a bank run, servicing ten banks in a hundred-kilometre radius. Given that the run finished in Belcowie, Wyatt figured the total snatch could be worth as much as $400 000.

It had to be worked from the inside. He needed to plan and watch, and that took time, so posing as a tourist or salesman was out—no tourist or salesman ever stayed in Belcowie for long. This way, as one of the grimy hundred and fifty, Wyatt wouldn't be noticed. And by the time the cops had got through interviewing a few hundred residents and construction workers next payday, he'd be long gone.

The siren sounded for lunch. Wyatt straightened the kinks in his back. He was tall and fluid-looking, with a hard edge that kept him out of trouble when the South Americans got rowdy. They were friendly, quick and sentimental, and he liked them, but some thought they had something to prove, and he could sense them watching him sometimes, looking side-on at his narrow, hooked face and loose, strong arms.

He crossed the shed and joined the Chilean mechanics at the stainless steel sinks. He measured hand cleanser into his palms from the dispenser and slapped it up and down his forearms and over his hands. Just then one of Leah's girls walked past the shed on her way to her caravan. The Chileans began to whoop and whistle, and one of them nudged Wyatt, but the woman didn't interest Wyatt. He was watching the Steelgard van, memorising all he could. When he hit next Thursday he wanted it to go like clockwork.

Steelgard had got slack, that was clear. They were based in Goyder, a rural city seventy kilometres away, and in all the years they'd been servicing the banks there had never been an incident to sharpen them. The van was a small, short-wheel-base Isuzu with external rear-door hinges and ordinary locks. But the van wasn't important. Wyatt wasn't interested in the van, only in the slack security.

First, there were no cops keeping an eye on things. Sometimes a patrol car from Goyder showed at pub-closing time, but only for thirty minutes and usually on the weekend. There was no guarantee that cops wouldn't show next Thursday, but they hadn't come for today's delivery, and Leah had never seen them come, so Wyatt was betting they wouldn't show.

Second, the camp was almost deserted. The only people populating the wasteland of concrete pipes, fuel drums, earth-moving equipment and temporary buildings were Leah's girls and a handful of clerks and mechanics. Everything would change at two-thirty, when the crews came in to clean up and collect their pay packets, but Wyatt intended to be a hundred kilometres away by that time next Thursday.

Third, the guards looked easy. Only two men, and they lacked that edge Wyatt had seen on his other hits. He noticed other lapses. Instead of one man unloading while the other stood guard, both unloaded. And Brava hadn't assigned anyone to help them.

Then, as Wyatt watched, the guards shut the van, lit cigarettes and strolled across to the canteen. They'd have lunch and come back to supervise while the pay packets were made up, but right now the money was in the care of just one man, the pay clerk.

Wyatt would have hit then and there if he'd had a gun, a partner and a fast car.

TWO

The set-up was exactly as Leah had described it.

Wyatt had turned up on her doorstep six weeks earlier, on the run from a Melbourne job that had gone sour. His cover had been blown, he was wanted for murder, he'd had to leave the state. A few addresses and a wad of cash were all he had in the world.

Her home in the Adelaide Hills had been in darkness the night he arrived. He prowled around it warily, looking at the doors and windows. The ground-floor curtains were drawn, but there was a window open in one of the two upper-level rooms that had been built into the steeply pitched roof. He knocked and waited. No lights came on but after a while he'd sensed that she was behind the door. 'Leah,' he said softly.

Her voice came low and hard. 'Yeah?'

'Wyatt.'

She had opened the door, noted his hunted look and his paleness, and stood aside to let him in. She didn't say anything, not even as he took out his .38 and prowled with it through her house. It was something he had to do, an instinctive thing, so she waited until he was finished.

'How long this time?' she said.

'Not long. A week, two weeks.'

'It's been five years, Wyatt.'

He nodded. He had no use for this, then realised a beat too late that it was mostly a joke. He smiled at her briefly, a sharkish twist of the mouth.

'Are you broke?' she said.

'Not entirely.'

She nodded. 'You're on the run,' she said. 'This isn't a job.'

Wyatt watched her for a moment. She'd been sleeping and was wearing a thigh-length black T-shirt. She had black hair, cropped short so that it spiked. She was small and compact-looking, and he remembered her round brown belly and how quick and elastic she could be. He felt calm and safe now. He put the gun away and placed his hands on her upper arms. Instantly her ironical expression disappeared. She closed her eyes and breathed out. She opened them again. 'Well, come on,' she said, almost irritably.

It was the next morning when they were in bed, which was a mess, that she'd told him about the Belcowie payroll.

'Godforsaken little place,' she said, 'in the middle of nowhere. Nothing ever happens there, except one day the government decides to put a gas pipeline through and the locals wake up to find a hundred and fifty randy construction workers living on their doorstep.'

'That's where you come in,' Wyatt said.

'Exactly. Fifteen hundred bucks a week and nothing to spend it on except beer and poker. I made Jorge an offer—I put a few girls in, you get ten per cent and a contented workforce.'

Wyatt leaned on his elbow and touched her. It was absent-minded, but she looked down her body, watching his hand. 'The money,' he said.

She flopped back. 'I stayed on for a couple of weeks, helping the girls get settled, laying the ground rules, kind of thing, so I was there twice when the payroll came in.'

'Details,' Wyatt said.

'Payday is each Thursday. The van arrives just before lunch. The security's not very good.'

Wyatt nodded, beginning to shape the job in his mind. 'Cops?'

'The nearest cop shop is an hour away. I never saw a single jack the time I was there.'

'What about the camp? Who's around when the money arrives?'

'Hardly anyone. The crews knock off about two-thirty on Thursdays to come in and pick up their pay, but the place is quiet until then.'

'How many guards?'

'I only saw two, same ones each time. They stay until the pay packets are made up, and leave about three o'clock.'

'The town?' Wyatt said. 'Witnesses?'

'The camp's along one edge of the town, in an empty paddock. From memory there's a bowling club and a few backyards opposite, that's all. It's a pretty dead place.'

Wyatt began to pay attention to her again. She laughed and wriggled. 'You like it, huh?'

'I'll check it out.'

'I can ask Jorge to give you a job there.'

His face had been tired-looking and distant, but now she saw it sharpen. '*No!* No links.'

'Suit yourself,' she said, stretching, closing her eyes.

A few days later she drove him down from the hills to the bus station in the centre of Adelaide. Buses going through to Broken Hill passed within twenty kilometres of Belcowie, so he caught one of those. He got off at a crossroads on a mallee scrub plain and started walking. A mail driver picked him up after an hour and dropped him on the outskirts of Belcowie. It was early afternoon. Wyatt knew motors and he looked strong and he could drive a truck. By four o'clock Jorge Figueras had given him a job laying pipes for $1500 a week.

THREE

Now, drying his hands and watching the camp dog cock its leg on the Steelgard van, Wyatt knew how the snatch would go. He would hit as soon as the money was unloaded and the pay office more or less unattended. Any later and he'd be dealing with armed men and a hundred and fifty pay packets. He had seven days to put a good team together and stash some cars between Belcowie and Adelaide.

'Hey, *gringo*, lunch.'

It was the repair shop foreman. His name was Carlos and he was standing with the other Chileans, waiting for Wyatt.

But Wyatt was concentrating. He stared at the Chileans as if they weren't there. The Chileans shrugged and turned away and set out across the dusty yard to the canteen.

Wyatt looked at his watch. Fifteen minutes later he left the shed and took a roundabout route past the site office and the front gate. He was still concentrating, fixing in his mind the timing and the geography of the town and the camp. Leah's girls worked from caravans a few hundred metres from the men's dormitories, in a corner of the camp screened from the town by peeling gum trees. The boundary fence went along the eastern edge of the town and the town itself straggled north and south for three kilometres. After that it was nothing but dry farmland and distant hills.

His attention was caught by a movement in a dusty lot opposite the camp. A month ago the lot had been vacant, and it would be vacant again when the camp moved on, but now it was a branch of Trigg Motors, a struggling car dealership based in Goyder. Half a dozen used Holdens were gathering dust under a string of sun-faded plastic flags, and a caravan annexe bellied in the wind. Trigg himself was there today, a short, ferrety man dressed like a grazier, pasting a sale sticker to the windscreen of a 1973 Kingswood. Trigg was always there on payday, when the South Americans had money in their pockets. Apparently he enjoyed haggling with them. Wyatt turned away. Trigg would see the snatch next week but he was no hassle.

Wyatt's next step was to get a fix on the driver and the guard. Just as he was approaching the canteen the driver emerged. Wyatt saw a big, soft, fleshy man, with large worried features crammed together on a small head. The name tag on the uniform said 'Venables'. Wyatt turned, watching him go. Venables grunted as he walked. He looked tight and knock-kneed, his vast behind stretching his trousers.

Wyatt had no interest in Venables, beyond the man's potential to foil a holdup, but then Venables did a curious thing: he didn't go to the pay office but out the front gate, across the gravel road and into Trigg's yard. He conferred with Trigg for a few seconds, then both men left the lot and walked along the road to the pub on the corner.

Wyatt heard a clatter behind him. Carlos emerged from the canteen. He tapped his watch and grinned when he saw Wyatt. 'Fifteen minutes, okay, *gringo*?'

Wyatt grinned back at him. '*Sí señor*,' he said, and he went into the canteen to get a look at the guard.

At three o'clock it all came apart.

Although the pipe-laying and trench-digging crews were back in camp and the showers were running hot and men were lining up outside the pay office, Wyatt was still in the repair shop, stripping a gearbox. Permanently suspicious and wary, he was the first to notice the upset. It started with the unmarked cars and vans. There were ten of them, all white. Half entered the camp, the other half took up positions around the perimeter fence.

Wyatt didn't know what they wanted but he did know his

prints and description were now on file somewhere, so he wasn't going to stick around to find out. His gun and most of his cash were at Leah's so he wasn't bothered about the few things in the locker next to his bunk. He stepped back to where he couldn't be seen and watched as thirty men got out of the cars and vans. There were plain-clothes among the uniforms, but what interested him most were the insignias on the uniforms. These cops were federal, not state.

Then a group of Chileans outside the pay office made a useless run for the gate. A scuffle broke out. Soon all the cops were involved.

Illegals, Wyatt thought. Fucking Jorge has been employing guys who've overstayed their visas.

He crouched in the shadows. There were a couple of Kingswoods across the road in Trigg's yard. Wyatt could hot-wire Kingswoods with his eyes closed.

FOUR

'I'm good for it, Ray, you know that,' Tub Venables said.

Raymond Trigg screwed up his eyes. He was lighting a cigarette and the smoke got him, every time. 'I know you are, Tub. The question is, when?'

The car dealer and the security van driver were in the front bar of the Belcowie Hotel, a dim, beery room with laminex surfaces and cracked brown linoleum on the buckled floor. It was two thirty and they'd been since one o'clock, Trigg nursing small glasses of Southwark Light while Venables soaked up pints of draught. The Chileans would be crossing the road with their pay packets soon, but meanwhile Trigg had to keep Tub Venables from falling apart. 'You got to be more responsible, my son,' he said. 'Five thousand bucks—it's a lot of money.'

'Interest,' Venables said mournfully. He sweated when he was scared. He was also leaning on the bar cloth, getting his elbows wet. 'I've paid back the principal, but you keep charging me interest on the interest. I'll never catch up.'

'That's how it works, Tub. Five thousand bucks principal costs you five hundred a week interest. The five thousand has to be paid back in a lump sum—like you can't pay five hundred interest and a hundred off the principal or something. I told you that at the beginning. You shouldn't have borrowed so much.'

Venables's face creased fatly in cunning. 'I could just stop paying.'

'Ah, come on, Tub. You know what happens if you do that.'

Venables looked gloomily back into his beer glass. He didn't like Trigg. Trigg was a short, scrawny bloke who tried to compensate for it with his moleskins, Akubra hat and elastic-sided boots, as if he owned a sheep station instead of a car yard. But he knew it wouldn't do to underrate the man, for Trigg also ran the local SP, loan-sharking and distribution rackets, and with the downturn in the economy he'd become mean and touchy. Hold out on him and he'd send in Happy Whelan, his mechanic, a mindless big thug who'd break your neck as soon as look at you.

'You drink too much,' Trigg said. 'You want to watch it. That and the horses and fast women, Tub, you'll keel over before you're fifty. I'll never get my dough then.' He poked the fat man. 'Joke, Tub, for Christ's sake.'

Venables looked up. 'All I want is a bit more time. I don't want fucking Happy knocking on my door.'

Ray Trigg's bloodless lips stretched in a smile. 'You're sounding like a cracked record, old son.' He looked at his watch. 'Shouldn't you get back to work? Your mate's going to be pissed off. I mean, someone could snatch the payroll.'

'Never happen,' Venables said, easing his buttocks off the bar stool.

He stood there, watching Trigg climb down. He felt a dangerous desire to lift the little man under the arms and deposit him on the floor. He hated Trigg's staved-in face, the neat little rabbit teeth on his lower lip, the elevator heels.

Trigg seemed to catch his thoughts. He looked vicious suddenly. 'The vans are booked in two weeks from yesterday, am I right?'

Venables nodded. Trigg's garage in Goyder had the servicing contract for the Steelgard vans.

'Pay me a thousand then, no less,' Trigg said.

He turned and crossed the room, nodding at the licensee and the only other customer, a farmer sneaking a quick beer.

'Something's going on over the road,' the licensee said.

Trigg paused. The licensee was wiping glasses and looking out the window at the camp beyond the vine-covered pub verandah.

The farmer turned to look. So did Trigg and Venables. They

watched, fascinated. There were white cars and vans every-
where and knots of policemen struggling with angry construction workers.

'It's a raid,' Trigg said.

As they watched, a tall figure loped unnoticed from a corner
shed, scaled the fence as if it were nothing, and dropped this
side of it. He seemed to land on the run. There was something
skilled and resolute in the way he moved.

Venables and Trigg pushed through the old-fashioned swing
doors. The road was empty. Shouts and struggling continued
inside the camp, but the man had disappeared.

Then they heard a car start up. It entered the road in a con-
trolled skid, fishtailed in the gravel, and sped past them, the
engine working hard. It was a big, dusty Ford and they had an
impression of intensity and jutting angles in the man behind
the wheel.

Trigg, seeming to swell, stamped his little heels. '*Bastard*. He's
taken the LTD.' He shook his fist at the receding dust cloud.
'You're history, pal.'

FIVE

The keys were in the ignition of Trigg's LTD so Wyatt took that rather than waste time hot-wiring one of the rust buckets in the used-car lot. He headed north from Belcowie, driving the big car punishingly, feeling it bounce and shudder on the torn-up roads. He lost control at one point, spinning around in gravel and slamming against a strainer post. It slowed him down. The side panel had buckled, scraping the front tyre, and he limped into Terowie, a small town on the Broken Hill road. General MacArthur had stopped there once, in 1942; that was all Wyatt knew about the place.

Within five minutes he had stolen another car. He drove south this time, keeping to the main road. In Riverton he stole a third car. The closer he got to Adelaide, the more civilised the landscape seemed to become. The towns were closer together, the farms less wind- and sun-blighted. But he was afraid of road-blocks. At Tarlee he headed across to Nuriootpa and wound through the small towns, wineries and sleepy tourist roads of the Barossa Valley. Then, hoping they'd think he was aiming for Melbourne, he turned south-east and drove to Murray Bridge. He dumped the third car there and caught an Adelaide train, getting off in the Adelaide Hills.

He walked the final ten kilometres to Leah's house, taking small back roads which were choked on either side with black-berry bushes. Soon his heart stopped hammering. The hills reminded him of the small farm on the Victorian coast which he'd been forced to abandon a few weeks earlier. There were the same orchards and fat white sheep, the same geometric patterns of roads, paddocks, hedges and townships. Only the sea was missing. He breathed in and out, almost enjoying himself.

He let the tension run out of his body and started to think about the chinks he'd identified in the Steelgard operation. Wyatt didn't take foolish risks. Having a shot at the Belcowie payroll now would be risky but he thought he could make it a calculated risk. He acknowledged the element of frustration in his motives, but frustration wasn't an emotion he had much time for.

Wyatt was forty years old. Respectable men his age were marking time until their retirement. The hard men his age were dead or in gaol. Wyatt was different. He'd never been burdened by doubt, uncertainty or personal ties. He worked from an emotionless base. He could cut to the essentials of a job and stamp his cold hard style on it.

The essentials of this job were clear—the Steelgard operation was vulnerable, at least on the Belcowie run. The guards were careless and lazy, the delivery itself unvarying and insecure. He'd have to change the how and the where, though. Belcowie and the Brava camp would be in a state of tension for the next few weeks.

A car changed down to first gear behind him and began to labour up the hill. He stepped off the road and into a clump of trees. The vehicle came into view, a faded green Land Rover with dogs and fencing wire in the back.

When it had gone, he continued walking. Ten minutes later he came to the little town where Leah lived. It was called Heindorf and revealed the German influence in its cottagey stone houses, painted wood trims and European trees.

He stood at the end of her street and crouched as if to tie his shoelaces. He couldn't see anything that shouldn't be there. The cars were the same ones he'd seen a few weeks ago. No one was about. He stood up, entered the street, and walked to the end. Leah's house was halfway along. Everything looked all right. He turned the corner. The street backed onto a small pine forest. He climbed through a wire fence, circled behind the first row of trees, and stopped at the rear of Leah's house. He checked for life in the neighbouring houses. No windows were visible, only fences and backyard fruit trees. It was early evening. Here and there a light was on.

Leah was squatting with a trowel at the edge of a strawberry patch when he cleared her back fence. He landed neatly and crouched, as still as a spooked cat in the twilight. She didn't seem surprised to see him; she merely stabbed the trowel into the black soil and stood up.

'It was on the six o'clock news,' she said, brushing her hands on her jeans.

'Immigration?'

She nodded. 'They detained eight of Jorge's Chileans.'

'Anything about me?'

'Only that one man had escaped in a stolen car,' Leah said. Then she looked bitter. 'I had to tell my girls to pull out. The feds were getting nosy.' She shook her head. 'It was a goldmine while it lasted.'

She was getting depressed. Wyatt knew her well enough to read the signs. She'd sometimes fall into a fatalistic blackness of spirit that might be triggered by some reversal but was never entirely absent from her makeup. She thought of her past as a yoke. She'd been on the game for years, and now she ran girls who'd once been like her. She believed that she'd be happy when she broke out of that pattern. She needed luck, she'd say sometimes. Luck and money.

'I've been thinking,' Wyatt said.

'That's what you're good at, Wyatt.'

He let it go. He said, 'I want another crack at the payroll. I need your help.'

He knew that she welcomed action when she got the blues. He watched her. Normally he thought of her as having the kind of grave beauty that didn't need a smile or other signs of life, but now she grinned. Her nose wrinkled. It altered her entire face.

SIX

The day started badly for Trigg and it got worse. First there was an article in *Cosmopolitan*. He'd gone into 'Cut and Dried' for a body-wave, add a few centimetres to his height, and he was under the dryer, flipping pages, when he came to 'Short Men—Are They Sexy?' Raelene had yanked him out before he finished the article but not before he'd read that because Alan Ladd was so short, Hollywood had shot all his love scenes with him standing on a box.

Then when Trigg walked back down the main street of Goyder, two people made cracks about the LTD getting stolen in Belcowie the day before, and his reflection in the shop windows showed that his body-wave was full of air, standing up from his head like it was in shock. His cuban-heeled elastic-sided boots seemed to expand to the size of footballs on his feet. He had the feeling the whole of Goyder was laughing at him. It got so bad that he stopped and bought a tub of Brylcreem, and back at Trigg Motors he plastered his hair down and saw clients without getting up from behind his desk.

But he'd asked the mayor to drop by after lunch. He'd have to stand up then—there was a lot at stake. She arrived at two-fifty, twenty minutes late, and he took her on a tour of the showrooms, service bays and car lots of Trigg Motors, calling her 'your worship'.

Then he took her back to his office. 'Coffee?' he said. 'Tea? Something stronger? I got sherry, gin and tonic, rum and coke?'

The mayor's cat's-arse mouth tightened. She seemed to sniff. 'I'm afraid I have to get back to chambers,' she said.

Trigg knew then that he'd lost, but still, he grew businesslike and clapped his hands together. 'I'll be brief,' he said. 'I've been in this city ten years. Trigg Motors is a pretty big concern, I employ a lot of people, plus there's all the other spin-offs for the local economy. The city's done a lot for me, now I want to give something back.'

'Mr Trigg—'

'Liberal endorsement for Central Ward next month,' Trigg cut in. 'As a Councillor I could do a lot for this city.'

The mayor had started to back towards the door. She was a neat little package in her formal spring suit, stiff hair and handbag, and Trigg wanted to push her over. 'Oh, I am sorry,' the mayor said. 'The Party's already got someone in mind for Central.'

'That was quick,' Trigg said, before he could stop himself.

'Mr Trigg, there are procedures. Long service to the Liberal Party, and so forth.'

Trigg wanted to say, *And old money. And brown-nosing.* He held it back and kept his voice even. 'Perhaps if I could address the local branch?'

The mayor stopped backing away from him and seemed to come to a decision. Her chin up, her back straight, she said, 'I think it only fair to tell you we can't afford to do anything, well, open to interpretation.'

Trigg's face changed. 'Spit it out,' he snarled.

The mayor flushed. 'The rumours... I'm sorry, Mr Trigg,' she said.

This time she reached the door and opened it and disappeared through it.

Trigg's right hand went up to shape and pat his hair. It came away slicked with Brylcreem. He checked in his desk drawer mirror and saw a gleam of oil on the tops of his ears. He wiped them with his handkerchief. He was churning inside. His debts were crippling him; business was non-existent. But try and expand, make the necessary contacts, and see where it got you. The old money had this town sewn up tight.

The call on his private line came soon after that. He heard

the STD beeps and then Leo Mesic in Melbourne was saying, 'You were down this month.'

Trigg went pale. Panic settled in him. He hated and feared the Mesics.

'Well?' the voice said.

Trigg tried to rally. After all, Melbourne was six hundred and fifty kilometres away. 'I was down last month and I'll be down next month. There's a recession on.'

The voice went on as if he hadn't spoken. 'You know how it works—every time you miss a payment or part thereof, you're deeper in shit.'

Trigg wanted to say, *Watch my lips.* 'What do you people expect over there?' he said. 'You tie me up with cars no one here can afford, they're using the farm ute till wheat and wool prices come good again. The guy subcontracting the pills, booze and the videos owes me twenty thousand. The kids have switched to sniffing Clag or something because they can't afford speed. I mean, what do you expect? You must be getting the same story from all your other mugs.'

While Leo Mesic responded to him, Trigg reflected that there wasn't much difference between an upright citizen cunt and a gangster cunt. They both squeezed you out. Neither gave you a break.

'...which comes to three hundred thousand you owe us,' the man in Melbourne said.

'Look, no offence, but when people here pay me what they owe me, I'll pay you what I owe you.'

People like Tub Venables, he thought. It was ironical—the Mesics had him paying interest on the interest, and he had Venables paying interest on the interest, and neither of them could pay. The only way I'll get anything out of Venables, he thought, is payment in kind.

Out of the hum on the line Leo Mesic said doubtfully, 'Maybe we can discount the cars.'

'That would help,' Trigg said, keeping it light.

Underneath it he felt sour and anxious. The Mesics had him where they wanted him—by the balls. Now that they'd got him to invest, they weren't about to let him buy his way out. The booze, videos and drugs were cheap, but he still had to pay up front. The stolen cars all had 'legitimate' paperwork but they were Mercs and Volvos and top of the range Toyotas that no one could afford any more. Would they let him sell on consignment? No way. He could run, but they'd track him down sooner or later.

'Three hundred thousand,' Leo Mesic said. 'See what you can do to reduce it.'

The line went dead, but the day didn't improve. Trigg's intercom buzzed a few minutes later and Liz in reception said, 'Sergeant King to see you. Shall I send him in?'

Jesus Christ, Trigg thought. 'Did he say what he wants?'

'Something about yesterday.'

'Has he found the LTD?'

'He didn't say. He just said can he have a word about yesterday.'

'Tell him to come in,' Trigg said.

At first Trigg thought he'd remain behind his desk, but then he thought you can't do that to a cop who's maybe doing you a favour, so he was standing at the window, looking out at acres of Volvos, Mercs and Toyotas, all unsold, all stolen, when King came in.

'Master of all he surveys,' King said.

Trigg kept his face even. King could be a sly bastard. Either he was being pleasant or he was saying he knew the cars were bent. Well, let him. Using the cover of pumping petrol for Trigg after school, King's son pushed dope to the town's riffraff.

'Fancy a Laser?' Trigg said. 'I can give you two thou off this week.'

'Speak to the wife,' King said. He was six feet tall, veined and stringy as a length of rope. Trigg had to cock his head back to see King's face. 'Listen,' King went on, 'we just traced your car.'

Trigg winced and shielded his face, miming apprehension. 'Break it to me gently, old son.'

'Smashed headlight, crumpled passenger-side wing.'

'The bastard. Where was it?'

'Terowie.'

'Terowie? He's heading for Broken Hill,' Trigg said. 'He'll go to ground there with all the other wogs.'

'Did he look wog to you?'

Trigg shrugged. 'These days your wog looks like you or me. You can't tell.'

'According to the blokes he worked with, he's not wog, he's Australian.'

'So why did he run?'

'You tell me,' King said.

They stood side by side at the window. Outside, Happy Whelan was washing an XJ6 in his overalls. He looked like an ox with a toothache. Acres of duco baked in the sun. 'With all the excitement there yesterday,' Trigg said, almost to himself, 'I thought maybe someone was trying to snatch the payroll.'

SEVEN

'Leah sent me,' Wyatt said.

The man wearing the overalls had a wedge of watermelon at his mouth. He was snatching bites from it as if Wyatt had a stopwatch on him. He spat out a pip. 'Leah,' he said, wiping the juice away.

'She said you could fix me up with a bike.'

The sign outside said Jap Job. The proprietor of Jap Job gestured with the watermelon at the motorcycle parts, tools and greasy rags that surrounded him. 'Bikes are my business,' he said.

'She said ask for one of your specials,' Wyatt said.

'Did she now?' The proprietor snatched another bite from his watermelon. He had long, tangled hair and a drooping moustache. There was juice on his chin. He chewed for a while, then pointed the watermelon rind at Wyatt. 'If ever your guts are crook,' he said, 'eat this.' He tossed it away then, dramatically, stood stock still and brought out a liquid belch. 'Better out than in.'

Wyatt was tired of this. 'Let me concentrate your mind,' he said, lighting a match and throwing it on the floor. It landed a metre away from a cut-down drum in which carburettor parts were soaking in petrol. He followed it with a second match.

The proprietor of Jap Job went white and rigid. 'It's concentrated, it's concentrated.'

'I want a bike that's good on the open road and across country. Something strong, fast and light. I want it today, and I don't want anything that can be traced to some semitrailer hijack.'

The man went sullen. 'It'll cost you.'

'How much?'

'Three thousand.'

Wyatt had money left over from the job that had gone sour in Melbourne, so he didn't quibble. 'What time?'

'Five.'

'Five o'clock,' Wyatt said, and walked back onto the street. Jap Job was a stone and corrugated iron shed in a side street behind the business centre of Gawler, a town forty minutes north of Adelaide. Wyatt walked back to the centre, found a hotel, and ate a mixed grill. It was the first mixed grill he'd eaten for five years. He'd thought they'd gone out of fashion. He asked for a glass of light beer with it. The barman managed to sneer without moving a muscle in his face. Wyatt supposed that the only light beer served in this pub was in the ladies' lounge.

He spent the afternoon exploring. He'd gone to Adelaide by bus and to Gawler by train and he was tired of sitting down. He liked Gawler. He liked the old stone buildings and the river, the town-and-country feel about the place.

At four-thirty he retrieved the backpack he'd stashed in a station locker and by ten to five he was at the rear of Jap Job. Easy Rider had looked like the sort of man who'd call in the Hells Angels to sort out his grievances, but there were no strangers about.

At five o'clock Wyatt came in the front way, his hands loose at his sides. There was a motorbike in the corner that hadn't been there before. The proprietor didn't greet Wyatt, only said, 'Suzuki Five Hundred. Clean as a whistle, climb Mt Everest.' Wyatt didn't care what sort of bike it was. He straddled it, to see how it would fit him. The engine felt warm, so he started it with the ignition key. It fired up, low and satisfying. He turned it off again.

'You want to test her?' the man said.

'I'll be back if it's no good.'

'I don't know where you come from, pal, but here you won't get far without a helmet.'

'Throw one in,' Wyatt said.

'It'll cost you.'

Wyatt paid the extra and at five-twenty he was riding out of Gawler with a black helmet on his head and the pack on his back. When he was clear of the local traffic he opened the throttle full out. He wanted to be on the back roads behind Belcowie before sunset.

The white line flashed by under him. A bike was better than a car for what he had in mind. He'd be covering rough ground. He'd need speed and manoeuvrability when he was in the open, and he needed a vehicle he could hide at a moment's notice.

The sun was low in the sky when he reached the crossroads where the Broken Hill bus had set him down a few weeks earlier. He turned off toward Belcowie, dropping his speed because the road surface was treacherous and this was the time of day when bone-weary farmers drove home in the centre of the road in utilities with bald tyres and faulty lights.

Wyatt had a specific place in mind. He'd spent a week with the surveyor when he first started work with Brava Construction, checking sight-lines across a small range of scrubby hills. They'd gone in along dirt tracks and followed fences and seen only kangaroos and nervy sheep the whole week, but there had also been an abandoned farm in there, tucked away in a valley between two arms of the range of hills. He wouldn't know how good the place was until he got up close, but he did know it had a north exit and a south exit and two exit lines was the first thing he demanded of any hideout.

'Why not rent a place?' Leah had said. 'That way we'd get somewhere comfortable and look legitimate.'

'Names, faces, paperwork,' Wyatt replied. He'd said it quietly, not looking at her.

'You're obsessive, you know that?' she said.

The shadows were lengthening now. Wyatt turned on the headlights, picking up a couple of rabbits and a cat on the prowl. Insects were mashing against the visor of the helmet. He came to a landmark he recognised, a roofless tin hut surrounded by pepper trees, and turned off the Belcowie road onto a smaller one. He slowed right down, steering the bike over channels that had been there since last winter or since the last time the council grader went through—and that might have been a decade ago. He was concentrating. He didn't want to miss the track that led to the farm. He had a nylon tent in his backpack, together with a camping stove and a sleeping bag, but he'd rather sleep in a shed than at the side of the road. He didn't want some mountain man turning a spotlight and a hunting rifle on him during the night, and he didn't want a crop duster buzzing him in the morning.

He got to the farm gate just as the sun was setting. Next to it was a stock ramp, sealed with a tangle of barbed wire. Wild oats were growing at the base of the fence and gateposts and choking the metal grid of the ramp. The track beyond it was stony so he was unable to tell if it had been used recently. He dragged the gate open, being careful not to flatten the weeds, and wheeled the bike in.

He left the bike behind a boxthorn hedge and approached the farm buildings on foot. It was a five-minute walk. There were trees and rocky outcrops between the buildings and the road gate. Wyatt hoped that these had muted the sound of the bike; if anyone was camped at the farm they might not realise that the bike had stopped.

There was sufficient light for him to see that the first farm building was an implement shed. It was empty, facing the next building, a hayshed constructed of gum tree logs and rusty iron. The roof, of mouldy, weather-stained thatch, had collapsed. The yard around the shed and the distant farmhouse was a mess. Empty drums, tangled fencing wire, engine blocks and rusty harrows and ploughs were trapped in the stiff, dry grass. A small tree was attempting to grow through the roof of an outside toilet.

Then he examined the house. The walls were standing and most of the roof was up. That was all Wyatt needed to know

about the farm—room for vehicles and a team of men.
He walked back to collect the bike.

EIGHT

That was Wednesday. On Thursday Wyatt woke with the dawn, feeling stiff and bruised from the hard ride the previous afternoon and the unyielding floor that had been his bed. He'd heard rats in the night. This morning there were rat droppings near the sleeping bag. He could smell dust and the damp staleness of the walls and floors. Outside, the sparrows and finches were making a racket, but he didn't mind that, and the sunlight was soft and warm.

His breakfast was black coffee, sweet and strong, and muesli bars. He explored the area around the house and assessed the surrounding hills. The farmhouse was set higher than he'd remembered it, which was good, for it gave a clear view of the approach roads. There was a way out of the valley behind the farm along a twisting, rutted track. The implement shed had doors on it and room for a couple of vehicles. The house itself was habitable enough to shelter three or four men for a few days.

Wyatt had a delayed getaway in mind. Instead of running, and risking roadblocks, they'd hide in the area until the heat was off. The roadblocks would come down after two or three days, and they'd make their run then.

He washed and shaved in a zinc bucket, put on clean jeans, a leather jacket and the helmet, and rode out of the valley. According to the road and ordinance survey maps that Leah had bought for him in Adelaide, Goyder was seventy kilometres from Belcowie, making it ninety kilometres from the farmhouse. Wyatt didn't bother with back roads. He headed for the bitumen and made Goyder well before the shops and banks had opened.

Goyder called itself a city, and reinforced the notion with parking meters, three sets of traffic lights and a pedestrian mall. There were branches of Myer and David Jones in the mall, and a convent, a high school, a TAFE college and a hospital on the outer edges. It had fast-food and video joints, and service stations on every corner. Trigg Motors sprawled over an entire block. There were coin barbecues and a Christ-in-the-Manger scene in the memorial park. Goyder was vulgar and it would have been smug if the local landowners had had more money to spend in it.

Wyatt found Steelgard on a street behind Trigg Motors. There was a motor accessories shop opposite, so he propped the bike outside that and watched the Steelgard place in the window reflections. The time was eight o'clock and Steelgard was opening its shutters and doors. He saw people go in the front door, and then the gate at the side was opened, revealing an open garage and a parking apron. As Wyatt watched, drivers got into three of the Steelgard vans and drove them out and across the street to the diesel bowsers at Trigg Motors.

Just then a pimply kid came along the footpath. He stopped next to Wyatt and unlocked the front door of the shop. He wore moleskins, desert boots and a skinny leather tie over a khaki shirt. He smiled at Wyatt. 'Great day,' he said.

'Sure is,' Wyatt replied. Although he still had the helmet on, he kept his face averted. Who knows, the kid might have a photographic memory.

'Help you with anythink?' the kid asked.

'Just riding through.'

'Fair enough,' the kid said, and he went inside and opened up the shop.

Wyatt fired up the Suzuki again, swung round so that he could see the Steelgard place more clearly, and rode out of the city.

He didn't know where else Steelgard went on Thursdays, but he did know there was only one road out for the van delivering the Belcowie payroll. He waited for it in a layby on the outskirts of Goyder. A fruit and vegetable stall was set up there, so he ate an apple while he waited. The land here was richer than around Belcowie. Small wineries and horse studs patterned the flats and nearby hills.

The Steelgard van went by shortly after eight-thirty. Wyatt gave it a minute, then tossed away the apple and set off after it. He stayed well back. He didn't use the headlight. If the driver was alert—and Wyatt had to allow for a reasonable degree of alertness—he'd see only a distant, intermittent shape on the road behind, if anything.

By the time the Steelgard van was nearing the end of its run in Belcowie, Wyatt had followed it for three and a half hours. It stopped at eight banks and two building society agencies in nine different towns. Each pick-up and delivery took ten minutes. There was only one other stop, at ten o'clock, when the driver pulled over in a busy town to buy takeaway coffee. The van kept to the speed limit, obeyed all the road rules and stayed on the main roads.

Between stops, Wyatt thought about the van itself. It was the same short-wheel-base Isuzu, with the same two-man crew he'd seen in Belcowie. The bodywork looked to be one-centimetre steel plate. The smoked-glass windows were probably bulletproof. The rear doors looked more promising. The locks were concealed but the hinges weren't. They could be prised off with the right tools. The ventilators also looked promising. If he could be sure that Steelgard was too lax to carry gasmasks, he'd try dropping tear gas down the ventilators.

He recalled other security van snatches that he'd pulled. There had been the time his gang came in underneath, forcing a way through the mesh floor of the van, and the time they'd forced a way through the engine bay to gas the driver. Both methods had worked, but required time and a great deal of effort, starting with detour signs to lure the van somewhere quiet, and experts to work the expensive, noisy cutting gear.

But you couldn't rely on using the same method twice. The security firms had got wise. Soon drivers were always varying the route and never straying off the main roads. If confronted with a detour sign they radioed in for the okay before taking it. The vans themselves became harder to penetrate. Wyatt had heard of concealed aerials in the wing mirrors, sirens that could wake the dead, sonar tracking signals and complete shutdowns, where the brakes locked and none of the doors would open.

He wondered if Steelgard had moved up to that kind of protection. He doubted it somehow. But that didn't mean it would be easy. He still had to find a way in. There was still the radio link the van would maintain with the Goyder base. There were still witnesses to consider. The main roads here couldn't be called busy, but even one car every five minutes was one car too many.

The solution to the problem of witnesses presented itself on the last stage of the Steelgard run. Wyatt was following the van along a firm dirt road that looped around to Belcowie when he saw flaring brake lights and a back-up of dust. The van was turning off the good dirt road and onto a lesser dirt road. It was taking a short cut.

Wyatt throttled back. He didn't go in but stopped to examine the van's tyre tread pattern in the dust. He would follow again next Thursday. If they used the same route he would hit them the following week.

The way into the money itself he'd worry about later. The van's radio was a different matter. He'd call Melbourne tonight, ask Eddie Loman to send him someone who'd have the equipment and know-how to jam it.

NINE

'Gabe?'

'Yeah,' Gabe Snyder said.

'Eddie Loman here.'

Snyder didn't reply for a moment. He was braking gently, the car phone at his ear, allowing the moron ahead of him to cut left into Waiora Road instead of Lower Plenty Road. Snyder didn't want to hit anything. His Toyota van was the latest model and it was full of the latest radio and cellular phone gear. He waited for the moron to get a few car lengths ahead and said, 'Eddie. Long time no see.'

Eddie Loman's voice faded in and out. Snyder attributed it to distance and to the hills in this part of Melbourne. 'Say again?' he said.

'Busy tonight?' Eddie Loman repeated, and this time his voice came through loud and clear.

'Well, you know, Friday,' Snyder said. 'Catch the action at the Cadillac Bar, maybe.'

'Can you drop in and see us first? I might have something for you.'

It was freaky. Snyder could hear Eddie Loman clearly now. He accelerated through the intersection at the corner of La Trobe University then slowed on the other side. 'La Salle Park Psychiatric Hospital' a sign said. Snyder looked at his watch. It was four o'clock, visiting time. There'd be a few cars in the grounds, perfect cover, just as he liked it. 'Six o'clock all right?' he asked.

Then the signal faded again. There was a crackle that he hoped was Eddie Loman signing off, and the line went dead. Snyder replaced the handset of the car phone and concentrated on his driving. His mouth dropped open when he did that. It was a large, damp mouth in a loose, pouchy face. The pouchiness helped to conceal the acne a little. The hair helped too. It was curly, salt and pepper coloured, and he wore it to his shoulders. In 1969 he'd been called up for national service in Vietnam. He'd opted for a radio course so he wouldn't have to fight, but the army barbers had still cut off all his hair. He'd spent the years since then making up for the indignity.

Normally he wore overalls, always dazzling white Yakkas, great-looking against the tan he kept topped up in the Lifestyle solarium. But he'd discovered, the first time he cruised the La Salle grounds, what a drag the overalls were, so today it was green Stubbie shorts, Reeboks and a T-shirt. He also wore Nepalese rings and bracelets, bought cheap from weekend stalls on the Esplanade.

He turned the Toyota into the hospital grounds. Lawns stretched for miles, interrupted by walking paths, seats, flowerbeds and clumps of European trees. Most visitors turned right, taking them to the main buildings. Snyder took the left fork, which circled the hospital perimeter. Staff and visitors rarely ventured where he was going.

He rolled down his window and listened. The Toyota echoed off the bluestone wall on his left and the belt of weeping willows on his right, sounding like a sewing machine. Snyder was disgusted. The trouble with all the greenhouse shit they bolted to engines these days was not only loss of power but also loss of a decent exhaust note.

Then Alice stepped out from the trees and waved. Snyder looked at his watch: four-fifteen. When he'd come here on Monday he'd said to her, 'I'll be back Friday, okay? Friday, *quarter—past—four.*' He'd said each word slowly and clearly, hoping they'd register but knowing they mightn't. After all, she was in here because her brains were scrambled.

But she had understood him, and here she was, four-fifteen, waiting for him. He stopped the van where it was screened from the hospital administration block by trees and watched her approach. Her hair had been washed this time. It floated free from her head like bits of spider web in a breeze. Her jaws were busy with chewing gum again. He'd smelt it on her breath on Monday, Juicy Fruit or something. She looked doped to the eyeballs again, her skin blotchy, a bit of dribble on her chin.

Forget the face, Snyder thought. Put a bag over it. He smiled at her through the glass and opened the passenger door. Jesus Christ. She was actually blushing and moving her shoulders around as if she was a teenager getting into her boyfriend's car for the first time. She'd been around, though. She looked to be about thirty. Now and then on Monday she'd almost made sense some of the time.

'Alice,' he said.

Alice got in and shut the door and slid across the seat and put her tongue in his ear and her hand inside the leg of his shorts. Snyder was glad he didn't have the overalls on. 'Did you bring them?' she asked.

Snyder played with her. 'Bring what?'

Instantly her arms went around herself, her mouth turned down and her eyes went ugly with tears. 'Smokes,' she said. 'Nice things.'

'Oh, that,' Snyder said.

'*Please.*'

'Smoking's bad for you.'

The mouth opened again and wailed, 'You promised.'

'Settle down,' Snyder muttered. He managed a smile. 'You're not being fair,' he said. 'If I give you nice rings and nice smokes, you have to give me something in return. It's not fair otherwise.'

It was amazing how easy it was to switch her off and on. She'd said on Monday that she'd been in La Salle for fifteen months. Snyder felt the shrinks should have done something for her in that time, but she was still fucked up. As he talked, he watched her face. A flooding look of relief and gratitude passed across it, followed by dismay, followed by a look of lust that was almost enough to turn him right off. Her hands and tongue started to go all over him as they had on Monday, and he told himself again, forget the face.

He showed her the carton of cigarettes inside the shopping bag in the back of the van. That set her going again. She climbed over the seat, pulling her pants off, tugging at his hand. Although he was only with her for fifteen minutes, the atmosphere was so hot and feverish that he was able to do it twice.

Then he pushed her out with the cigarettes and a $12.95 necklace. He drove back to the main entrance, keeping his eyes open for hospital security. As usual, there was none.

By six o'clock he was in Eddie Loman's back room, hearing about a job he was needed for over in South Aussie.

The interesting thing about it was, Wyatt was behind it.

TEN

Snyder could see that Eddie Loman was hedging. Loman wouldn't meet his eye, and he kept rubbing his gammy leg. Snyder waited, testing him, then said, 'Aren't you missing something?'

'What?'

'There's a fucking contract out on him.'

Loman's face twisted. 'You heard.'

'Course I fucking heard. Twenty grand to the guy that fingers him.'

Loman continued to rub his leg. The movement pulled his trousers up, revealing pink plastic skin. He'd lost the leg ten years ago in a collision between a getaway car and a divisional van. Maybe he still gets ghost feelings in it, Snyder thought.

'I mean,' Snyder continued, 'you begin to wonder why Wyatt's putting an outfit together if it means all these guys are going to know where he is. You'd have to be mad, right?'

He watched Loman pour beer into their glasses and put the bottles under the coffee table. There were three bottles there now, Melbourne Bitter, resting on their sides. Loman had neat habits. His living quarters behind his hardware supply business looked to be tacked together from mismatching building materials and fire-sale furniture, but there wasn't a speck of dust or a bad smell in the place.

Loman swallowed beer from his glass. When he put the glass down again it was fair and square on a coaster with an Aborigine painted on it. 'Actually,' he said, 'I don't think Wyatt knows.'

'We come to the crux of the matter. You could've told him when he rang last night, but you didn't.'

Loman looked up. 'Wyatt knows how to look after himself.'

'Cut it out, Eddie. You were going to charge him a finder's fee for lining me up for this job of his, then dob him in for the twenty thousand. Am I right? Bit of a cunt act.'

Snyder was enjoying himself. He didn't care much for Loman. Loman supplied experts and equipment to people who had big jobs on, and Snyder had got some work that way sometimes, but you couldn't actually like the bloke. That grey face and smoker's cough, the sense of decay on the inside. Plus, Snyder didn't like being cheated. He didn't like it that Loman was intending to earn himself an extra twenty thousand without cutting anyone else in on it.

'Eh? Bit of a shitty thing to do to the old Wyatt? Not to mention the danger to yours truly. What if this hired gun comes after Wyatt when I'm in the firing line, eh? Answer me that.'

Loman's face worked in worry. 'I would've told him. I thought, you know, this job of his is out in the bush somewhere, he'll be safe there till it's over. Then I'd give him the word, kind of thing.'

Snyder nodded. 'Oh, right, I'm with you now. You're not after the twenty grand reward.'

'Not me. Wyatt's—' Loman struggled '—well you don't exactly call Wyatt a mate, do you, but he's a good client, kind of thing.'

Snyder's loose face seemed to tighten and he leaned forward. 'How much?'

'Pardon?'

'What's he paying you? What am I worth?'

Loman rubbed at his leg. 'Fifteen hundred.'

'What's the job?'

'He didn't say, except it's big.'

'And there's a radio he wants jammed. Did he say what I get paid?'

'A percentage. Not a fee, a percentage of the take.'

Snyder grinned then. 'Correct me if I'm wrong—you only get fifteen hundred bucks, I stand to get tens of thousands. I can see how a bloke might feel a bit put out about that. He might want to grab a bit more. Not you, though.'

A flush showed under Loman's grey skin. 'I didn't know you and Wyatt were such good mates.'

'We're not. I'm a professional, he's a professional. We just do our jobs. We don't get greedy, rock the boat, work behind another bloke's back.'

'You've made your fucking point,' Loman said, leaning back in his chair. The fabric was slippery brown vinyl and it seemed to fart under him. He shifted again as if to demonstrate that it was the chair, not him.

'I mean,' Snyder went on, 'Wyatt's good value. He does the right thing by blokes like you and me. You'd have to be a real bastard to shop him to some hired gun down from Sydney.'

'All right, okay?' Loman said. 'You've made your point.'

'That would be a cunt act,' Snyder said.

ELEVEN

Letterman did contract work for the Sydney Outfit now but he still looked like a cop. There was no need for him to wear grey suits any more, but he felt wrong in anything else. He was tall, solid and punchy-looking, an effect that was ruined if he put on jeans or corduroys and a casual shirt. He felt he looked soft in clothes like that—like a suburban bank manager on a Saturday morning.

He threaded a navy blue tie under his collar and leaned toward the mirror to knot it. He was indifferent to the hairs in his ears and nostrils. They were indicators of his vigour and perpetual anger. So, somehow, was his balding skull. He remained close to the mirror. He was in a motel room in Melbourne that might have been designed for midgets. The mirror was too low, the bed too short, and he always had to duck his head to get it wet in the shower stall.

Although he felt relaxed, his face looked tired and unimpressed. When he was working, it looked alert and unimpressed. He was forty-six, doing what he did best, and had never felt better. The Outfit paid him a retainer that equalled his old detective inspector's salary, plus a flat fee for each contracted hit. There was $50 000 coming his way when he found Wyatt and knocked him off. The Outfit wanted Wyatt bad. Wyatt had hit them where it hurt, killing their Melbourne head and destroying their biggest Melbourne operation.

Not that he'd be easy to find. Letterman was approaching this as if he were still a cop. For a start, the trail was cold. Most breaks in a case come in the first twenty-four hours, but Wyatt had dropped out of sight six weeks ago. Apparently he was a pro, so he'd avoid his usual haunts; in fact, he was probably interstate somewhere, keeping his head down. But he'd caused so much heat, done so much damage, aroused so much media and police attention, that the Outfit hadn't dared send Letterman to Melbourne before now.

Other factors were working against him. First, Wyatt didn't want to be found, meaning he'd cover his tracks, use forged ID or alter his appearance. He wouldn't be found wandering the streets like some old pensioner who'd lost his marbles. Second, Letterman couldn't call in favours from other cops anymore. Third, the Outfit wasn't very popular here in Melbourne. In the four days since his arrival, Letterman had been spreading the word around, $20 000 to the one who fingers Wyatt, but so far not a whisper. Wyatt was a Melbourne boy too, so that probably had something to do with it.

But the twenty thousand dollars would work eventually. Letterman knew how it was with police work—ten per cent detection, ninety per cent fluke. He'd arrested crack dealers who'd traded in the VW for a Mercedes sports, wife murderers who'd given themselves up, burglars at the scene, holdup men who'd been dobbed in for the reward. Letterman was patient. Twenty thousand was a lot of bread.

Other things were in his favour. Unless they were incredibly loyal in Melbourne, Wyatt wouldn't be aware that the Outfit was after him. He'd be expecting cops, not contract hitmen. And crims don't change their spots. Wyatt would surface sooner or later. He'd want to pull another job. He would need money soon, and he was a big-score crim, the kind who puts together a gang, and you can't stay out of sight when you do that. Until then Letterman would take it step by step, like a cop. The usual routine: where was Wyatt last seen? Who saw him last? Who are his known associates?

He put on his suit coat and left the motel. The other thing about a suit is, you can hide a gun under the coat and get at it easily, where you can't if you're wearing a shirt or a jumper.

His Avis Fairmont was parked outside the motel room, its

long snout overhanging the tyre-stop. He made the usual
checks before getting in. He noted that there was no one in the
space behind the front seats, then opened the boot lid gingerly,
checking for wires before opening it fully and searching for a
mercury electrode. Finally he examined the driver's seat for
pressure bombs and checked for wires under the bonnet. The
car was clean. He put on the black hornrims he wore for driving, got in and backed the Fairmont out of the motel carpark.

He left St Kilda and drove down the Nepean Highway to
Frankston. There he cut across to Shoreham and found the post
office. It was attended by an elderly, watery-eyed man. 'I work
for the *Courier Mail* in Brisbane,' Letterman said. 'I'm doing a
story on the gangster who lived near here.'

'You mean Warner?' the postmaster asked.

Letterman nodded. He'd been reading back issues of the
Melbourne newspapers and knew Wyatt had used that name.
He'd also obtained photocopies of the police identikit picture.
He pulled one out and showed it to the postmaster. 'This him?'

They both examined it. According to the police artist, Warner had a thin face, loose shortish hair and bleak features.

'Not a bad likeness,' the postmaster said. 'I tell you what, we
were flabbergasted. Seemed a nice sort of a bloke, kept to himself, kind of thing. No one here had a clue.'

Letterman put the picture away. Everyone had a clue now,
though. It was quite a story, front-page stuff. Gang warfare,
the headlines said. Organised crime elements from Sydney
battling it out with local criminals, several of whom had been
shot dead. Police were looking for a man who called himself
variously Warner, Lake and Wyatt, last seen at his farm on the
Mornington Peninsula.

'I'm putting together a story about the hidden lives of people
like him,' Letterman said.

The postmaster pursed his lips and looked out of the window. Letterman wasn't perturbed. The guy was trying to say he
was canny, you couldn't put anything over on him. 'A Brisbane

paper, you say?'

'That's right,' Letterman said.

'You heard about it up there?'

The way to this bloke's heart was pride. 'I'll say,' Letterman said. 'It was a bloody big story.'

The postmaster beamed, then looked regretful. 'There's not much I can tell you, though.'

'For starters, did he get any mail? Readers like to know about that kind of thing. You know, letters from girlfriends, letters from overseas, letters from interstate, stuff like that.'

The postmaster shook his head. 'Like I told the police, he might've posted letters, but he never received any. People don't write like they used to. They use the phone these days.'

Letterman thanked him and got directions to Wyatt's farm. The house was sealed up. All the grass needed cutting. The dirt track showed no sign that vehicles had been along it recently. Wyatt is long gone, Letterman thought, and he won't be coming back. Letterman said as much to a neighbour, an angry-looking farmer. 'You'd be mad, wouldn't you,' the man demanded, 'to try coming back? We were pretty upset about the whole thing. If he *did* show himself now, no one would give him the time of day.'

Letterman got back into the Fairmont. It had been a wasted trip, a long shot that hadn't paid off, and he'd stepped in cow shit and pulled a thread of his suit on a barbed wire fence. He hated the bush, didn't know why anyone would want to live there.

Frustration brought on his indigestion, and during the long drive back to Melbourne he let himself reflect upon the past couple of years. They'd said he could make Commissioner one day. He'd come up through the ranks, and he'd done law and accounting part-time in his younger days. He'd had his own detail in the vice squad, and been second in command in the drug squad.

But you don't get anywhere waiting for information, so he'd

built himself a good network of snouts, turned a blind eye where necessary, picked up the odd suitcase from a station locker.

Then came the whispers; that he'd corrupted junior officers, made deals with underworld figures, assaulted witnesses. He faced them all down. Then he was charged: conspiracy to murder, conspiracy to pervert the course of justice, attempted bribery. They didn't have a shred of evidence, their witnesses suddenly got cold feet or went on holiday, and Letterman had walked, but eighteen months ago the police tribunal had sustained five out of eight misconduct charges against him and he was given the boot.

He'd cleaned out his desk and gone home. That evening the phone had rung. It was the Outfit. You scratched our back in the past, they said, so we scratched yours, dropped a few quiet words in a few ears. So how about it? Want to continue doing what you're good at?

As he drove through Moorabbin Letterman pictured again the hate on the faces of the cops who'd tried to put him away. He fished a Quick-eze out of his pocket and chewed on it. His belly rumbled and the pain eased. What he most liked about this job, apart from being his own boss, was there were no more logbooks, no more manuals, no more working by the book.

St Kilda Junction was coming up. Letterman crossed into the left lane, ready to turn into Barkly Street and his motel. Change his suit, clean the shit off his shoes, then back on the streets.

Known associates. When everything had blown up in Melbourne six weeks ago, three names surfaced: Wyatt, Hobba, Pedersen. Hobba was dead. Wyatt was the reason for all this in the first place. That left Pedersen.

TWELVE

'A woman is good cover, Wyatt. Think about it.'

Wyatt thought about it. Leah had a sharp mind and she liked to use it. He'd noticed that five years ago, when she'd done some background work for two jobs he'd pulled in Adelaide. And now she was bombarding him with ideas for the Steelgard hit. Most of them made sense. All the same, he didn't want her to be involved at an active level.

'I've got a stake in this, Wyatt.'

He stared at her face. Intelligence and a kind of fury were animating it. Her eyes were alive. Her fists, clenched on her dining room table as she leaned toward him, looked impatient and ready for action.

Then her eyes narrowed. 'You don't think I can do it.'

Wyatt gestured irritably. He didn't speak.

'What, then?' she demanded.

Wyatt wasn't going to tell her that the job had become messier, costlier and more difficult than he liked. It had started off as an uncomplicated snatch, but the federal police raid had changed all that. He forced a smile. 'We need someone useful here on the outside.'

She ignored the smile. 'I'll be more useful there with you than back here. I can drive, shop, take photos, whatever.'

Wyatt nodded slowly. They were drinking—his last drink before he started work—and he could feel his resistance slipping away. He watched Leah watching him. Her body was still but gave an impression of being charged with energy. She was frowning faintly, and her eyes were restless.

'I could keep watch,' she continued. 'You'll need someone on a radio to tell you when the van enters the short cut.'

'Maybe.'

'Think about it.'

Wyatt regarded her calmly. He didn't speak.

She went on. 'Tell me more about this guy coming from Melbourne.'

'He knows about locks. He's also good with radios. The van will be equipped with long-range VHF on a constant band. We'll need to jam it. With any luck the Steelgard base will think it's a signal weakness.'

'But you don't know yet how you're going to break through to the money.'

'There's always a way. I'll set up a camp first.'

'You'll brainstorm the job first,' Leah snapped.

Wyatt rarely got angry with other people. He didn't get close enough to them for that. Their problems and opinions didn't interest him. The sort of people who angered him were the punks he'd sometimes worked with, whose grievances and ignorance put his life at risk. But he felt angry now. He felt it rising in him.

Something in his face betrayed it. Leah blinked and jerked her forearms back from the table. She picked up her wineglass and drained it.

'You don't like working with a woman,' she said.

But that wasn't it. He didn't like to be rushed. The answers always came to him when he was alone, concentrating hard. Just now he didn't feel like concentrating. He was aching after riding the Suzuki all over the state and the wine made him feel sleepy and he wanted Leah to have her mind on him, not the job. Then he caught himself. He didn't like that sort of thinking in himself.

'Okay,' he said, 'we'll brainstorm the job.'

'Bribe someone on the inside,' she said promptly.

'Like who? The driver? The guard? What will you ask them to do? What if they talk? Do you actually know anyone at Steelgard?'

'No.'

'No, but if you approach them they'll soon know you. Next idea.'

'We put up a roadblock. When they stop we get the keys off them and open the back.'

'A roadblock may come into it,' Wyatt said, 'but it doesn't mean they'll give us the keys. First, they don't ride together in the cab. The guard rides in the back, which is a separate unit sealed off from the driver's cab. Usually the guard opens from the inside. And I note that you said "we".'

He said all this coldly and rapidly. Nevertheless, Leah grinned. She was enjoying herself. After a while, Wyatt grinned too.

Leah's smile faded. She was thinking. 'What's the company policy when staff lives are in danger?'

'These firms don't want anyone getting hurt or killed. It costs them too much in compensation and bad PR. The money's insured. They tell their employees, if it comes to the crunch, give in.'

'So we drag the driver out and hold a gun to his head so the guard sees it, or we hold up a stick of dynamite and tell the guard if he doesn't open we're blasting the doors.'

'The driver and the guard are linked by an intercom,' Wyatt said. 'We can jam their radio, but we can't jam that. As soon as something goes wrong, the driver will warn the guard.'

'So?'

'So there could be a whole range of emergency shutdown procedures we don't know about. Steelgard's employees are slack, we know that, but the vans could be high-tech all the same. They might be fitted with door and brake locks that can only be opened by someone from their base office. They might be fitted with time locks. You never know. We have to expect things like that. Breaking through that sort of gadgetry takes time, effort, equipment.'

Leah was silent. Then she said, 'So there's no easy way in.'

'There might be—we won't know till the day itself. What

I'm saying is, we have to be prepared for good-old fashioned force—cutting gear, blasting with nitro or C4 plastic, whatever. An effective, time-honoured, noisy, time-consuming, attention-grabbing method.'

Her face went rueful and she reached out and touched the back of his hand. 'Don't be like that.'

'Like what? I'm telling it like it is. We sit in the middle of the road for twenty, thirty minutes, an hour, cutting our way in, hoping no roo shooters or local cops come along.'

She grinned. 'Or we cut our way in somewhere else.'

'Where?'

'The hideout.'

'The hideout. How do we get to the hideout if we can't even get into the van and they've got some sort of complete shutdown in force?'

Leah poured more wine for them both, dragging it out, enjoying this. 'We cart it there,' she said.

There was a pause. He began to smile. 'A breakdown truck or a low-loader,' he said. 'And someone to operate it.'

She smiled back at him. 'I'll just make a phone call.'

She left the room and went into her kitchen. Wyatt sipped his wine. She wanted to protect her sources, so he didn't intrude. All the same, he felt vulnerable. Not about the fact that Leah had a say in things now, or about the quality of her opinion, but because he felt cut off from the people he normally worked with. He'd have to watch his back. He didn't know Leah's sources or if they could be trusted. He tried to tell himself this job was no different from all his others, when he had to rely on people like Eddie Loman for men and equipment, but it didn't help. Eddie Loman was as capable of selling him out as one of Leah's anonymous sources, but at least he *knew* Loman, knew where and how to find him. And Loman knew Wyatt—knew that if he crossed Wyatt he could expect a bullet that had no second thoughts attached to it.

Leah was dialling. An extension telephone sat on a coffee

table in the corner of her dining room and it tinkled fussily as she dialled. Wyatt counted—nine digits, long distance. He heard her say, 'It's me, Leah,' and then her voice went muffled. He didn't try to listen in on the extension. The best he could do for the next two weeks was keep his back covered.

He started to think about the truck. It was a good idea. It had the kind of neatness he admired. The problem was, how would they transport the van on the back of a truck without being noticed? The answer came to him and it was as neat and simple as Leah's initial idea. Brava Construction. Brava Construction's distinctive vehicles, pale blue with a snorting black bull on each door, had been churning up the mid-north roads for so long now they were part of the landscape.

Leah came back into the dining room. She was wearing black tonight and looked good in it. Black 'fifties skirt, black tights, embroidered Cambodian waistcoat over a black T-shirt. Her expression was light and cocky. She knew she was in now—she knew she would be there on the day. He realised that he liked her. He wanted her. This was his last drinking session until after the job, so it was partly the alcohol, but only a small part. 'Well?'

'It's all arranged. I was given a name. We go to see him tomorrow. He'll be expecting us.'

'Tell me about him.'

'According to my contact the guy we're going to see knows heavy vehicles. He's also pulled semitrailer hijacks in the past, he's a good mechanic and he's reliable.'

Wyatt pushed his chair away from the table and began to stand. 'Don't,' Leah said. The voice was low, almost a growl. Wyatt sat again.

She came around the table and stood looking down at him. She knocked her knee against his. Then she straddled him and when he put his hands under her skirt she arched her back. Five years ago she'd liked to do that. She'd been in the game then. He knew about it. It hadn't bothered him. It hadn't been

an issue. He wasn't curious about who she was when she was
with her clients, or why she did it, or what those other men
were like. It was business, that's all. Somehow she'd known he
wasn't the type to get bothered about what she did. And she was
too smart and careful to catch anything.

'Wyatt?' she said.

'I'm here.'

'Do you still go away every year?'

'If it's been a good year. Just lately, the pickings have been
poor.'

'But not with this job. You could be in Tahiti this time next
month.'

She was asking to go away with him. He didn't know about
that. He stroked her with his fingers and her back arched.

THIRTEEN

The next morning when the commuter traffic had eased they took the winding freeway through the hills and down into the city. Leah's driving was smooth and fast, no messy braking or swerving. Once they were out of the hills, Wyatt watched the traffic, the everyday commerce of the suburban streets. He did it automatically. It was as though these banks, payroll deliveries, office safes and jewellers existed only for him.

At Victoria Park racecourse he was reminded of a job he had on hold, to snatch the gate receipts at a big sporting event someday, some place where the security had been allowed to get slack. Leah skirted the vast parklands of the city. Boys were jogging around the playing fields of Prince Alfred College. Schools like this were never called by their full names. They were always Prince's, King's, SCEGGS, PLC, and it was always assumed that you understood the reference.

Wyatt's self-possession and control, his height and grace, had fooled people in the past. They mistook it for arrogance and good breeding. He'd once been asked, 'Were you at Scotch?' These schools, the people who sent their kids to them, spelt money, and Wyatt had set out to get some of it. It wasn't anything personal with him. He had no time for hatred or envy. Emotions like that used up energy and warped judgement. With Wyatt it was simply this: they had money, he wanted it, so what was the best way of getting it?

Leah turned onto Main North Road in Enfield and the city turned ugly. Sunlight blazed from windscreens and chrome in the used-car lots, and massive plastic chickens, hamburgers, tennis racquets and spectacles were bolted above the shop-front verandahs. Leah braked hard, swearing as a kid in a panel van swerved in front of her. The bumper sticker read 'Don't Laugh—Your Daughter Could Be In Here'. That's an old one, Wyatt thought. In fact, the whole city seemed to be about five years behind the rest of the world. Leah braked again, for a bus this time. Diesel exhaust hung in the air behind it and soon the oily fumes were fouling the air in the car.

'I always forget how shitty it is down here,' Leah said. 'I'm spoilt living in the hills.'

'Bushfires,' Wyatt said. 'Developers. Feral cats. Herbicide on the blackberries.'

'Ha, ha.'

A few blocks before Gepps Cross she turned left into an industrial park. 50% *leased!* screamed the signs along the fenceline. Grass grew to chest height around the empty buildings. Wyatt counted four stripped cars on the forecourt. Airconditioning ducts, packing cases and empty pallets were stacked along a steel-mesh fence.

'Here?' he said.

'It's the address I was given.'

Leah followed the main drive past the large front buildings and around behind them to a block of six smaller sheds and wholesale outlets. Three were vacant. The others were a hose and tap supplier, a cane furniture manufacturer and a small transport business. The transport business was at the end of the row and there were two vans parked outside it. A prissy script on the door of each van read 'KT Transport, Express Service to Country Areas'.

'Keith Tobin, esquire,' Leah said. 'No job too small.'

She parked the car and they got out. A man was on his back under one of the vans. He wore desert boots. He was tapping metal on metal and the soles of the desert boots twisted and turned in sympathy.

'Mr Tobin?' Leah said.

The boots were still. A muffled voice replied, 'Who wants him?'

'You got a phone call from a mutual acquaintance. You were told to expect us.'

Tobin was not sharp. The boots appeared to be taking in what Leah had said. After a while, the man slid out from beneath the van and stood up. 'Got you now,' he said.

Wyatt watched all this, hoping it didn't mean that Tobin was bad at his job. He saw a vigorous man aged about thirty, dressed in overalls. There were small blue tattoos on his forearms. His hair was cropped short, and a bushy moustache sprouted under his pitted nose. He was loud and cheerful, had vacant eyes in a lively face, and looked, Wyatt thought, exactly like a test cricketer. As he watched, Tobin stripped off the overalls, revealing brief green shorts, a blue singlet and long stretches of healthy-looking skin. Then Tobin put on sunglasses with mirrored orange lenses and said in a rapid mumble, 'Come in the office.'

Wyatt looked around once before following Tobin and Leah. If there was anyone who didn't look right hanging around, he'd pull out immediately. He saw no one. He went in.

The office was a mess. Ring-folders and crumpled invoices and receipts littered the desk and floor. There were beer cans on the window ledge. Wyatt didn't want to waste time. He didn't wait for Leah but said, 'Have you got form?'

Tobin took off the sunglasses. 'Sorry?'

Wyatt waited. It was the only thing to do. The seconds ticked by while Tobin got the question worked out in his head.

'Not me, mate,' Tobin said finally. A sullen expression replaced the open, empty look he'd started out with. 'What's it to you, anyroad?'

'You can drive heavy vehicles?'

Now Wyatt was speaking Tobin's language. 'No worries.'

'A low-loader, car transporter, something like that?'

'Yep.'

'Are you booked up this week?'

'Why? What's this all about? I was told you had a job on.'

'What about next week? Got any work on that can wait till later?'

Tobin looked sulkier. 'I'm not exactly swamped.'

'What about family, friends?' Leah asked. 'Anyone who's going to wonder where you are if you're away for a few days?'

'Nup. You better start fucking telling me what the job is pretty soon or you can fuck off, okay?'

Leah seemed to know what she was doing. Wyatt let her handle it. 'What are you doing this Thursday?' she asked. 'Any chance you can make a run up north?'

'Suppose. What's it to you?'

'We want to show you something. Do you deliver to Burra?'

'Every week. There's a bloke there owes me for a case of Scotch, five hundred smokes, videos...'

Leah nodded. 'We'll meet you there. Thursday, ten o'clock.'

'Listen, I'm getting pissed off with this. Time's money. If you want a pro you got to pay for it, and I want something up front.'

'Nothing up front,' Wyatt said. 'All your expenses will be paid and you get a cut of the take if you come in on this. Same terms for everybody.'

'How much?'

'Between fifty and a hundred grand.'

'Each?'

Wyatt nodded.

Tobin whistled. Then he jerked his head, indicating Leah. 'Is *she* in this?'

'Have you got a problem with that?'

'Well, I mean, you know.'

Wyatt turned and walked to the door. 'Okay, that's it, we find someone else.'

'No, hang on, mate, hang on,' Tobin said. 'No offence. Never worked with a bird before, that's all.'

'One thing,' Leah said. 'I'm not a bird.'

'Gi's your name, then.'

We're pushing him too much, Wyatt thought. He feels that

he's giving but getting nothing in return. 'Take it easy,' he said
calmly. He gave Tobin their names and described the job.
'Okay?' he said. 'Are you in so far?'

'Security van?' Tobin said, making a click of awe with his
tongue. Then he made a show of frowning hesitation, as if he
was a pro and the job had holes in it. 'The paint job'll have to
look right.'

'Yes.'

'Well, look no further,' said Tobin expansively. He pointed
through the window. 'See them vans? Painted them myself.
Duco, lettering.'

Wyatt inclined his head admiringly. 'Classy.'

Tobin thrust out his hand. 'Count me in,' he said.

Wyatt shook it, thinking there was muscle here and not much
else. But the job demanded muscle too, and if he could run the
operation so it was tight, the weaknesses wouldn't matter.

FOURTEEN

Letterman watched as Pedersen came out of his house and got into a Range Rover. The Range Rover looked new. He started the Fairmont, ready to follow Pedersen. He was reminded of the job a security firm had offered him when he was dismissed from the force. They wanted his detective skills, they said. They'd pull strings and get him licensed as a private investigator, and he'd start on $700 a week. The money was okay, but the work wasn't. Letterman knew about private investigators. They went into the game thinking they were Spensers or Cliff Hardys but soon went sour from boredom. Being a PI meant living in a car and working half a dozen cases at once—tailing wives and husbands, checking credit and employment records, drinking thermos coffee while workers' compensation claimants ran around on tennis courts, maybe getting out of the car sometimes to guard an exhibition of furs in David Jones. Stuff that for a joke.

The Range Rover's rear lights came on, the right one brighter and whiter than the left. Letterman had been tailing Pedersen for two days now. On the first day, when Pedersen stopped at a TAB to place a bet, he'd broken the brake light lens with a stone. He hadn't known then if Pedersen would go out at night or not, but if he did, the broken light would make him easier to tail.

Pedersen pulled away from the kerb. Letterman waited half a minute then pulled out after him. On Nicholson Street, where the traffic was heavier, he settled in two car lengths behind the Range Rover, keeping the bright tail-light in view.

So far today had been a repeat of yesterday. Pedersen had slept until lunchtime, spent the afternoon going to TABs, a pub and a brothel, taken Red Rooster chicken home for dinner, and

gone out again at eight o'clock. Last night Pedersen had driven
to King Street in the city. Letterman had watched him park the
Range Rover illegally, put on a black leather jacket ten years
out of date, and try to get into one of the clubs. He'd been re-
fused admission there and at another club a few doors along.
Letterman saw him gesture angrily at the bouncers in each
place. All the bouncers that Letterman had ever known were
ex-crims with records for violence, so Pedersen had been lucky
not to have his head kicked in. Not that Letterman blamed the
bouncers. Pedersen didn't look right. He had a prison pallor, a
jumpy manner, bad taste in clothes. And he looked almost mid-
dle-aged, too old for the King Street clubs.

Tonight was different. Tonight Pedersen drove to a pub in
Fitzroy. It had a blackboard on the footpath advertising mud
wrestling. That sounds about right, Letterman thought, watching Pedersen park illegally again and go in.

Letterman didn't follow straight away. He switched off the
engine and turned the radio to a talk show on Radio National.
With any luck he'd hear that some poofter had jabbed the New
South Wales Police Commissioner with a syringe.

Later Letterman turned on the interior light and scribbled in
his notebook. He had a complete record of all Pedersen's movements over the past two days, and they added up to one thing,
in his view—Pedersen was still living off the proceeds of the job
he'd pulled with Wyatt six weeks ago, the job that had wrecked
the Outfit's Melbourne operations.

He also had telephoto shots of Pedersen going in and out of
pubs, TABs and a brothel called Fanny Adams. He'd used up a
whole roll of film and had it developed at a one-hour place, the
sort of place that has a high turnover and no curiosity. Some
of the photos would go to the Outfit. They demanded before
and after shots of all contract hits. But the photos were also
groundwork. Letterman liked to make a study of his targets
before he hit them. He intended to hit Pedersen at home—he
hadn't decided how, yet—but if something went wrong and

he couldn't manage it, he'd go through the photos again and familiarise himself with Pedersen's other haunts. He hoped it wouldn't come to a hit in the open. The Outfit stipulated that in getting rid of loose ends like Pedersen he should attract as little attention as possible.

He turned off the interior light again, locked the Fairmont and crossed the road. He loosened his tie and untucked an edge of his shirt front before he entered the pub. He spotted Pedersen immediately, without appearing to look at him. The mud wrestling had just finished and the air carried a pungent layer of sexual hate and bitterness beneath the smoke, noise and splashed beer. Pedersen himself looked jittery and frustrated. Rather than front up to the bar, Letterman grabbed an abandoned glass with an inch of beer in it and slumped like a regular at a corner table. He didn't look directly at Pedersen. He didn't look directly at anything other than the floor. He kept Pedersen in his peripheral range. The Pedersens of this world, Letterman thought, can smell cop, even ex-cop, the instant they make eye contact.

Letterman stayed there for an hour. He ordered a glass of beer from a passing topless waitress at one point and endured another mud-wrestling match. A live band played between shows. Someone seemed to be selling speed and Buddha sticks.

Then Pedersen got ready to go. It looked like being an extended departure—he was clapping the shoulders of other drinkers who'd been ignoring him all evening—so Letterman left first. He crossed the road, got into his car, and settled a hat on his head. It probably wasn't necessary, but he didn't want Pedersen puzzling about where he'd seen the bald man in the Fairmont before.

As Letterman watched, Pedersen crossed the road unsteadily, U-turned in front of a tram, and sped north with a faint tyre squeal. Letterman waited for the traffic to ease, then followed him. Pedersen cut through to Nicholson Street and went north along it. He'd been drinking heavily and it showed in his driving. Just my luck, Letterman thought, if he gets pulled over for drunken driving. He lost Pedersen at Brunswick Road when Pedersen ran a red light, but it didn't matter, Pedersen was going home.

Letterman got to Pedersen's house in Brunswick in time to see the Range Rover's rear lights go off. He pocketed a Polaroid camera, got out and ran silently across the road and behind the Range Rover. It was a narrow street, dark, and Pedersen didn't hear him coming. When Pedersen let himself into his house, Letterman pushed in behind him. He pushed the door closed, hearing the lock click home, and took out his knife.

Pedersen spun around, then flattened his back to the wall in shock. His breath was beery. Letterman raised the knife and touched the blade tip under Pedersen's jaw, watching with interest the gulping motions in Pedersen's throat. He said softly, 'Maxie.'

Max Pedersen gulped again. 'Who are you?'

'You don't want to know that, Max,' Letterman said. He used Pedersen's first name deliberately. It gave him an extra advantage over Pedersen, who didn't even have a last name to call him.

For the next two minutes Letterman said nothing. Instead, he put his head on one side and then the other, turning the blade tip under Pedersen's jaw. The hall light flashed on the steel.

The silence began to work. It always did. 'What do you want?' Pedersen asked. 'Just tell me and I'll do it. You want money? I got some in my wallet.'

Still Letterman said nothing. He would let the silence do its job, then fire the hard questions so they hit like punches.

He shouted the first one. '*Where is he?*'

Pedersen winced. 'Who?'

Letterman said nothing. He waited, then asked softly, 'Where is he?'

'Who? I don't know who you mean.'

Almost a caressing whisper this time: 'Where is he?'

'Who?' Pedersen pleaded. 'Only I live here. Who do you

want?'

Letterman stood back at arm's length and nicked Pedersen's neck with the blade. When he spoke it was bleak and fast: '*Wyatt.*'

Pedersen's hand went up and came away with blood on it. He looked at it and then at Letterman, as if the world was spinning too fast for him. 'Wyatt?'

Ideally Letterman would have another man helping with the questioning, one to hurt the subject where it wouldn't show, the other to offer a way out of the fear and pain. '*Where is he?*' he repeated.

'Wyatt doesn't live here,' Pedersen replied. 'This is my place.'

Letterman was gentle and smiling again, but the knife was beginning to make a crosshatch of nicks on Pedersen's neck. 'I know that. I want to know where he is.'

'I haven't seen him for weeks,' whined Pedersen.

This was clearly the truth. Letterman had known it all along really, but still, he greeted it with total disbelief, another move that usually got results. 'Bullshit! You're working with him again.'

'No, promise, no,' Pedersen protested. He was close to tears. 'I swear I haven't seen him. He got in strife and cleared out and no one's seen him.'

'Let's say I believe you. I don't, but for argument's sake, let's say I do. If he cleared off, where would he go? Has he got some bird stashed away somewhere? Does he like to poke little boys in Manila? Maybe he's got an old mum over in Perth or something?'

Pedersen began to get his courage back. This maniac didn't want him, had nothing against him. 'I hardly know the bloke. He keeps to himself. One or two big jobs a year, then he drops out of sight again.'

Letterman smiled again and let the light flash on the blade. 'You work with him.'

'Only the once.'

'You were with him on his last job.'

Pedersen nodded reluctantly. 'Yes.'

'You stepped on some toes with that one,' Letterman said.

Letterman always used a thin blade. Thin blades slide in easily, avoiding needless hacking and cutting. He always held the knife flat and horizontal, and used a single, direct thrust. When he went in from the front he aimed for the carotid artery. A tough sheath of muscles protects it, and that's why the thrust has to be strong. He finished with a wriggle to sever the artery, removed the blade, and watched Pedersen slide, twitching, to the floor. It was quick and clean, one of the many things that separated Letterman from the amateurs.

He photographed the body, let himself out and drove back across the city to his motel in St Kilda. On the way he thought about the nature of luck in his profession. Although his leads had amounted to nothing, he believed that it was important that he'd followed them. It could mean good luck would come his way. He might hear something about Wyatt when he least expected it.

That was why he wasn't surprised to find a 'While You Were Out' message under his door. It told him to expect a phone call. The caller would ring every hour until midnight, and again the next day, starting at seven in the morning. Letterman looked at his watch just as the phone rang. Eleven pm. The voice on the other end said he knew where Wyatt was.

FIFTEEN

The fountain near the Gertrude Street lights, the caller had said, and Letterman was now watching it from behind a tree. He was in the southern area of the parkland attached to the Exhibition Building, on the city's edge. The time was five minutes to midnight. The caller said twelve-thirty, but Letterman was staking the place out first, looking for anyone who didn't belong there. A tramp was sleeping on a bench near the duck pond and another was under an elm, swigging from a bottle in a paper bag, but otherwise the area was deserted. Now and then kids and lovers walked through the park, pausing to watch the splashing water before moving on again.

Lights were strung around the Exhibition Building, and if he half-closed his eyes Letterman could see its shape picked out in pinpricks of light. A Japanese tour party had been in the park when he arrived, taking flash photographs of the possums. They were gone now. A pathetic-looking student wearing an old coat had passed by him twice a few minutes ago, but Letterman had growled, 'Got a problem, pal?', scaring him away.

At twelve-thirty a man approached the fountain and stood with his back to it. Although the light was poor, Letterman could see him clearly enough to know that this was his man. 'I'll be wearing white overalls,' the voice on the phone had said. Letterman saw a stocky man, standing confident and alert, the light making his long hair glow. There appeared to be rings on the man's fingers and chunky sneakers on his feet.

Letterman remained where he was. This was a good place for a meeting—the noise of the fountain would provide some cover if the informant was carrying a wire, there were plenty of exits and places to hide, and it was dark. But he knew that

darkness was no protection against fancy cameras and tele-
scopic sights. He wore a rudimentary disguise—the horn-rims,
his hat brim low, his collar turned up—but knew that wouldn't
stop a bullet in the back. There were plenty of people who'd
want to give him one. Yet the set-up *looked* okay.

He stepped out from the tree. The contact had devised a stupid recognition signal, but he went along with it. 'Excuse me,
I'm looking for the hospital.'

The contact jerked his head around, recovered, and pointed
toward a building opposite the city corner of the park. 'Over
there.'

Letterman left the shadows completely and joined the man
at the fountain. He said softly, 'What do I call you?'

'Snyder will do. You're Letterman?'

Letterman nodded. 'What have you got for me?'

'Not so fast,' Snyder said. He sat down on the lawn near the
base of the fountain and rested his forearms on his knees. 'Let's
talk this over.'

Letterman looked down at the bushy head for a few seconds,
then sat with Snyder. 'There's nothing to talk over. You tell me
where to find Wyatt and I pay you twenty grand.'

'It's not that simple. How do I know you're good for it? That's
the first thing. Second, I won't know exactly where Wyatt is until I make contact with him.'

Letterman stared at Snyder. He didn't like the man. Snyder
looked lumbering and dissipated and too pleased with himself.
Letterman felt an urge to slide the knife in, or slice off the ab-
surd hair. 'You're telling me he wants you for a job?'

Snyder nodded. 'Over in South Aussie somewhere. I fly out
first thing Monday morning.'

'He's meeting you?'

'Eventually. I fly to Adelaide. I take a taxi to the bus station.
There's a ticket waiting. The bus takes me up the bush somewhere. Now, that's all you're getting from me, pal, till I see the
colour of your money.'

Letterman ignored him. 'The bush? What sort of job?'

'Maybe I'm not getting through to you. This isn't a freebie, you know. I want something up front, and I want it now. The rest you can pay me when you see him, that's fair.'

Letterman removed the black horn-rims and cleaned them. 'Look at it from my point of view. I've been to South Australia plenty of times, I don't need to go again. Especially if I'm being set up, the man from Sydney making a fool of himself, walking into a trap, kind of thing. Give me something to go on, something specific.'

The last tram rattled by on Nicholson Street, a hundred metres away. Letterman saw the lights go out and on again at the centre of the intersection. He realised that the sound of the traffic was constant, even at this late hour. The air was getting chilly. He felt tired. Killing Pedersen had been a release, but now he felt tense again.

'All right, look,' Snyder said. 'It's some sort of payroll hit, that's all I know. He asked Eddie Loman to send him someone who knew about radios and stuff.'

'When's the hit?'

'Next Thursday.'

'Where's he meeting you?'

'Place called Vimy Ridge.'

Letterman took an envelope from his pocket. He didn't mind paying twenty grand to find Wyatt and he didn't mind paying an advance on it. What he minded was letting Snyder state the terms. 'Here's two thousand,' he said. 'Show me Wyatt in the flesh and you get the remainder.'

'You think you've got me, right? You think this way I'll be sure to get on that plane. Well, I was going anyway. I want a cut of this job. You can pop Wyatt when it's done, not before, okay?'

'In other words, I follow you and wait.'

'Yeah,' Snyder said, 'staying out of sight till I give the word.' He stiffened. 'Shit, cops.'

Letterman glanced up casually. Two young policemen had

entered the park from Nicholson Street and were walking toward them. They were carrying torches.

Letterman made his voice loud and slurred. 'The goodness is in all of us. The Lord Jesus taught me that. Have you looked inside yourself for the goodness?'

Snyder was reasonably quick. 'You're up a gum tree, mate,' he said, punching Letterman lightly on the upper arm. 'A flagon's the only place you'll find goodness. G'day,' he said, when the policemen drew near.

Both policemen grinned and continued along the path. Letterman watched them. Now and then they flashed their torches into the shadows. Soon they were out of sight somewhere on the southern flank of the park.

'Loman,' he said.

'What about him? You know him?'

'We've met. The question is, I asked him to pass the word around about Wyatt, so why didn't he tell me himself?'

'It's a mystery, all right,' Snyder said.

SIXTEEN

After meeting with Tobin, Wyatt and Leah went back to the car-yards on Main North Road and bought a twelve-year-old Holden utility. Wyatt wanted a vehicle that wouldn't attract too much attention out in the bush.

The next day they went shopping at supermarkets and army disposal stores before driving north to the hideout. They bought four camp stretchers and sleeping bags, a two-ring camping stove and fuel, enamel cups, disposable plates and cutlery, two shovels, a portable shower, a chemical toilet, lanterns, candles and tinned and dried food. Everything was going to be buried before they left the farm. Wyatt didn't intend to leave a single clue that they'd been there—no tracks, no garbage, no equipment that might identify them or tie them to the Steelgard hit.

They also bought four radios. Snyder was supplying a powerful unit to monitor the Steelgard van, but Wyatt wanted hand-held VHF/FM transceivers for communication in the field. He bought marine-band transceivers, assuming that no one in the bush would be listening in on that band.

The next few days would be a waiting game—waiting for Thursday, when they would show Tobin the layout, waiting for next Monday to meet Snyder, waiting for the Steelgard hit itself. It didn't matter that Snyder would miss the trial run. What mattered was feedback from Tobin. Would Tobin think it feasible that the Steelgard van could be carted away? Would he be able to find them a truck that would do the job? Would the narrow roads pose a problem? Were the sheds at the farm too small?

Wyatt lived with these questions in the early part of that week, not because he wanted to but because Leah was there. She was keyed up, anxious to do the job, looking at it from all the angles. Wyatt was calmer about it. He knew what the problems were, but they couldn't be answered until Tobin saw the layout, so there was no point in worrying until then. When he was working, Wyatt was concentrated and deliberate in all he did. He knew how to wait. He became remote and self-contained, which people often interpreted as arrogance. It was as if a small, chilling draft came off him. But he knew he had this effect on people, and because it was Leah there with him, he made an effort. He looked thoughtful when she raised objections about the job. He discussed the ins and outs with her. It kept them going. It kept up the harmony.

Not that they didn't have plenty to do. Leah made shopping runs into neighbouring towns—never the same town twice—to buy daily essentials like milk, eggs, bread, butter, fruit, meat and vegetables. While she was shopping Wyatt explored the possible exits from the farm. If something went wrong with this job, if they had to get out in a hurry, it would not be by the road leading to the property. That's where the trouble would be coming from.

First he checked the track leading back into the hills. He followed it all the way. At times it seemed to peter out, but he always picked it up again. It wound along the valley, around the edge of the hills, and eventually came out onto a secondary road on the other side of the range. He confirmed his earlier impression that it was passable to most vehicles.

But it wasn't the only exit. If both roads were ever cut off there were the hills themselves. An agile person could make good progress on the smooth slopes. The grass wasn't too high or dense. The main danger would come from hidden quartz reefs, rabbit holes and tussocks, all of them ankle-sprainers. There was also a reasonable degree of cover—the grass itself, creeks and erosion channels, rocky outcrops, solitary trees, their trunks rubbed smooth by forgotten sheep and cattle. From time to time he climbed to high ground. He was making a mental map of the area, marking topographical features, roads, neighbouring farms and the tin-hut corner, but being high up also gave him a sensation of unconquerability. He put it down to the clean, perfumed air, the blue and olive hills, the wind in the tossing grasses.

At other times Leah made him lie with her in the sun. When he was working he tended to forget about sex for long periods, so when she drew him by the hand and began to undress him, he would blink, surprised and gratified.

They also made two survey trips of the district. They had the maps, but maps are never sufficient. Wyatt couldn't work without pictures in his head. He liked to know about culverts, road signs, bends hidden by trees or farm buildings, overhanging branches, road edges churned and eroded by heavy vehicles, stretches rendered slow or impassable by potholes, sharp stones or washaways.

On Thursday morning they drove to Burra, a town that had grown prosperous on Merino wool after the copper mines had closed down. It had started as a cluster of separate townships on low hills, but they had amalgamated over time. The houses were built of local stone. Huge gums grew along the creek. Two-storey pubs with wrought iron verandahs and vines faced the town square, and the Cornish miners' cottages in the back streets had been tarted up for the tourists. There were two tourist buses parked outside the tiny museum when Wyatt and Leah arrived. A short distance away they found Tobin.

He was leaning against his delivery van, a bulky Ford painted iridescent blue, its doors and side panels decorated with gold curlicues. He was smoking, watching the locals through his orange lenses. Wyatt noted the way Tobin ignored the men. He was interested only in the women. When a woman walked by, he took the cigarette from his mouth and swivelled his head after her, his mouth hanging open. Leah saw it too, as they got out of the ute and approached him. 'Lovely bloke.'

'We're not interested in his personality,' Wyatt said.

'I am. The other day I could feel his eyes all over me. He's the sort who has sweaty hands.'

Tobin saw them approaching and stopped lounging. He threw down his cigarette and grinned. All Wyatt could see of Tobin's face were the grin, the cricketer's moustache and the reflection of himself and Leah in the orange lenses.

It's all psychology, Wyatt thought, working with men like Tobin. Talk their language and you're halfway there. 'Good run down?' he asked.

Tobin slapped the side of his van. 'Home to here in just under two hours,' he said. 'I already unloaded.' He counted on his fingers: 'Case of Scotch, latest release videos, souvenirs for the Tourist Centre.'

Wyatt looked at the van. The windows were smoky black; he couldn't see inside them.

'What time we getting back here?' Tobin asked. 'I got to deliver spare parts to a car place in Goyder this arvo.'

'About twelve-thirty.'

Tobin rubbed his hands together. 'No worries then. Let's hit the road.'

They squeezed together into the Holden utility and left Burra heading north-west. It was ten-thirty. At eleven o'clock they picked up the Steelgard van in Vimy Ridge, Steelgard's last stop before Belcowie. They tailed it out of the town, staying well back. The traffic was sparse, as it had been the previous week. The only road dust was coming from the van ahead of them.

'What do you think?' Wyatt asked.

Tobin was sitting against the passenger door on the other side of Leah, his head inclined toward the windscreen. Wyatt was aware of Tobin's excitement. He's getting a kick out of this, he thought. The van, the money, Leah's leg against his.

'What do I think? I expected a bigger van. This is going to be easy.'

'You can shift it all right?'

'No worries.'

'What if it shuts down—motor, brakes, locks, electrical

system?'

'Cut the brake lines and winch her in,' Tobin said.

He turned to face Wyatt as he said it. His back was against the door now, and he'd extended his arm along the top of the seat. His fingers were curled close to Leah's shoulder. Wyatt felt her move away from him.

'The next problem is,' Leah said to both of them, 'will the short cut be too narrow to take a truck?'

Tobin was an uneducated man. Like many men who work at practical jobs, he relied on physical gestures to supplement speech. Wyatt glanced away from the road for a moment, to see how Tobin would answer this question, and saw an elaborate play of shoulders, mouth and hands, Tobin's way of saying, 'You got me there.'

Ahead of them the dust cloud swirled and changed direction. Good—the van was using the short cut again. Wyatt waited for ten minutes before he turned in after it. They followed the track to where it met the main road again, four kilometres north of Belcowie. Wyatt stopped. 'Well?'

'No worries,' Tobin said.

He said it again thirty minutes later when they showed him the farm buildings. 'No worries. You could hide a bloody ship in here.'

He grinned at them. He had the orange shades on. Wyatt knew he was looking at Leah's breasts. 'So,' Tobin said, 'am I in? Is it a goer?'

'That depends. We still need a low-loader or a breakdown truck, one that can't be traced back to us.'

Tobin actually tapped his nose knowingly. 'Let me take care of that. So, am I in?'

Wyatt nodded.

Tobin stuck out his hand and shook Wyatt's enthusiastically. Then he put his arm around Leah and squeezed her. It was brief, as if it meant nothing, but he looked at Wyatt while he did it, and Wyatt knew the gesture meant everything.

SEVENTEEN

On Friday afternoon Trigg said, 'What do you mean, too expensive? Don't you kids get pocket-money anymore?'

The kid was about seventeen. He wore a prefect's uniform. His name was Wayne and he was Trigg's main supplier at the high school. 'I'm just telling you what they tell me,' he said. 'The speed's too expensive, so's the dope.'

'In my day kids had paper rounds, they mowed lawns, washed cars. Too fucking slack. These days if they're not hanging around the mall they're in Mooney's—'

Trigg broke off. If the kids were in Mooney's playing the pinball machines, how come Mooney kept holding out on the seven hundred and fifty bucks he still owed? Fucking everyone in Goyder was welshing on their debts.

'Fucking slack,' he repeated.

Wayne drank from the Southwark stubbie that Trigg had given him. He let Trigg rave on. The fact that Trigg was bent didn't mean that he wasn't like a parent when it came to what kids did these days. Half smiling at Trigg, Wayne said, 'Some kids are doing all right money-wise. The ones with a few dope plants. They charge less than you do.'

Trigg closed his eyes. It just wasn't worth the hassle. By the time he'd paid Wayne and the others, and allowed subcontractors like Tobin some leeway on what they owed him, he never had enough to meet the interest payment on his Mesic debt. He would have to start coming down hard on a few people.

'So if that's all...' Wayne said, putting down the stubbie and retrieving his satchel from behind the door.

Trigg attempted a smile. 'You're in a big hurry. Why don't you stay a bit longer?'

Wayne knew what it was about and his face shut down. He swung the satchel at the level of his knees. 'I have to get home.'

Trigg patted the two-seater couch. 'Just ten minutes.'

Wayne took charge. He dropped the satchel on the floor again and sat next to Trigg. He trailed his fingers absorbedly over Trigg's knee.

'You've had a haircut,' Trigg said.

Wayne shrugged. He kept up the movements of his hand.

'I suppose your girlfriend likes it?'

'Now, now, Raymond,' Wayne said. With the subdued light, the closeness, and the choked breathing, the air in the room was charged and avid. 'It hurt me last time,' he said.

'Oh, babe, you should've told me. We'll do it another way.' Ten minutes later Wayne said, 'Ten minutes,' and he was out of Trigg's house within sixty seconds.

Trigg made his phone calls then. He felt clammy. He picked at his clothing as he talked.

'Mooney?' he said. 'You're not getting any younger.'

'I can give you a couple of hundred,' Mooney said apologetically.

'What do you do there, anyhow?' Trigg demanded. 'Let the kids play the machines for free?'

He cut the connection and dialled a different number. 'It's Trigg. You're not getting any younger.'

The voice on the other end seemed to come through a mouthful of food. There were chewing noises and then a clearing cough. 'You've got me. You might as well repossess the car.'

Repossess the car? Jesus fucking Christ, Trigg thought, no one's buying cars to begin with. 'I'd hate to leave you without wheels,' he said. 'What say I come back a bit with the interest? Could you pay me, oh, a thousand by next month?'

'No good, sorry. The bank's taken my cheque book away. They're letting me stay on because they can't sell the farm. But they've seized me new plough, the wife's microwave—'

Trigg cut the connection. He was about to dial again but he

felt fouled underneath and went into the bathroom, stripped off, and had a shower.

It was five o'clock. He changed into clean moleskins, a checked shirt, a khaki tie decorated with the wool symbol, and a kid's sports coat bought in Myer's, and returned to the Trigg Motors showroom. His day wasn't made any better by seeing the wrecked LTD on a trailer at the back of the lot. He walked across to the pumps. Sergeant King's kid was slipping a foil packet to a couple of railways apprentices driving a panel van. He stood back till the transaction was over, then came closer. 'I'm getting a new shipment in tonight.'

'I've still got half the last one,' the King kid said.

'Not you as well?' said Trigg in exasperation.

Just then a school bus pulled in for diesel on its way back from a run through the surrounding farmland. Trigg turned away in irritation and went into the showroom. Liz was packing up to go home. Trigg checked the time: five-thirty. He sighed and went into his office, wanting badly to crack someone's skull open.

He picked up the phone, flipped open the rolodex, and dialled. 'This is Ray Trigg. Is Tub Venables still there?'

'Just leaving work now.'

'Ask him to pop in and see me first, will you?'

Trigg hung up and sat down in the chair behind his desk. It was fully ergonomic, with levers for raising, lowering, tilting. Coasters on the bottom. Lower-back support that followed you as you moved. In this chair, Trigg sat high behind his desk. The best six hundred bucks he'd ever spent.

A trick of the light illuminated Tub Venables as he appeared at the Steelgard gate and looked both ways before crossing the road. Trigg watched the fat driver approach, noting the body language. Scared shitless. A useless bit of useless blubber, all piss and wind.

Trigg knocked on the glass. Venables started, looked even more scared, and came around the back way. Trigg waited. A few seconds later, there was a knock on the door.

'Don't fucking stand out there,' Trigg yelled.

Venables came in. He shut the office door behind him and stood as if fearful of the vast stretch of carpet separating him from Trigg's desk.

'Come closer, old son.'

Venables advanced across the carpet, taking small steps. He stopped at the desk's edge. 'Look, I know—'

'Do you, now? So why give me a hard time? You think I haven't got better things to do than chase up welshers all the time?'

'It's not easy. My daughter's braces—'

'Plenty of kids lead fulfilled lives with buck teeth. But go on, let's hear the rest. I need a good laugh.'

'The granny flat's working out more than I thought. At least five thousand more.'

'Shove the old bitch in a nursing home.'

'So I haven't got the thousand I owe you,' Venables concluded.

'What I don't like,' Trigg said, 'is fucking cowardice. You've been avoiding me. You get your mates to tank up your van, I never see you, you must go in and out of work through the back door, you're never in the pub.'

'The wife—'

'The wife's broken your balls,' Trigg said. He stood up. 'I want you to come with me.'

'Pardon?'

Trigg rounded his desk and made for the door. 'Come with me.'

He led the way out of the office and across the used-car lot. He tapped his knuckles on the bonnet of a newish Honda Legend. There was another shipment coming in tonight, one Merc, one Saab. Why the fuck they couldn't send him Corollas or Commodores, he didn't know.

'In here,' he said.

They entered the service bay, a long, low structure that smelt of transmission fluid, grease and touch-up paint. Happy

Whelan was there, and Venables fell apart. 'Give us a chance,' he said.

Trigg ignored him. 'Hap,' he said.

Happy Whelan had an undertaker's face on a massive, bandy-legged, top-heavy body. His movements were slow, his mind was slow, but he could conceal rust patches and pack noisy differentials like a pro, and once started on something he was hard to stop. 'Yeah?' he said.

'Let's see if your new mallet's got any bounce in it.'

'Say again?'

'Bring Tub over here,' Trigg said, 'and we'll do some panel beating on him.'

Happy grabbed Venables by the upper arms and pushed him to where Trigg was standing next to the benches and wall-mounted tools at the rear of the shed. 'Place his thumb down there,' Trigg said, pointing at the top of the bench.

The front of Venables's trousers were wet. He didn't speak, just closed his eyes and swayed a little.

When the blow came he opened them, and groaned and went limp. Happy held him up. 'Not much of a bounce,' Trigg said, looking in mock surprise at the head of the mallet. He dropped it on the floor, its steel head striking a gouge in the cement, and reached for Venables's hand. 'You're going to have a nasty black nail there soon, old son.'

Venables was moaning, looking sick. Trigg stroked the back of the injured hand, letting the tips of his fingers brush across the thumb nail. Blood was welling under the nail. 'The pressure's building up,' Trigg said. 'We should do something about that. Hap, put Mr Venables's thumb in the vice. Not too tight.'

'No,' Venables said. He was helpless and rubbery on his feet.

Trigg waited until the thumb was ready, then took a Stanley knife down from its bracket on the wall of tools. It had a sharp, pointed blade. Happy used it for trimming upholstery.

'Your poor thumb,' he said, and he bent over it and began to pick a hole in the centre of the nail. Venables went white but watched, fascinated. In fact, Trigg was doing him a favour, but it all looked like the end to Venables.

Suddenly the blade cut through to the blood. It spurted out, then beaded, and Trigg said, 'Now, isn't that better?'

'You bastard.'

'One grand, this time tomorrow, when you bring the van in for servicing.'

'I haven't got it. I'll pay you some other way, anything you like, but I haven't got it in cash.'

Trigg began to push Venables out of the shed in a series of bitter shoves. 'You might live to regret that offer. Bugger off out of here.'

Then he stopped. A car transporter was outside, jutting half across the street as it backed in, the reversing signal beeping. The sight unhinged him, bringing back the pain. A Saab and a Mercedes, both newish, both black. Not only didn't the locals buy expensive models any more, they didn't buy *black* ones, not where the roads are dusty three-quarters of the year and muddy the rest of the time. And another batch of pills and videos that no one wanted.

EIGHTEEN

The more Letterman thought about it the more pissed off he felt about Loman. Loman knew about Wyatt but hadn't said anything. Loman had made him look foolish.

The feeling grew after his meeting with Snyder. He'd settled in at the motel to wait until the flight left on Monday morning, but he'd made the mistake of reading an 87th Precinct novel and that had been the last straw. He had to do something about Loman.

On Sunday evening he backed the Fairmont out of the motel car park and drove to a service station on Beaconsfield Parade. Here he bought two one-litre containers of engine oil. He drove out of the service station and turned left into a dark, narrow side street. He parked the car, got out, poured the oil into the nearest stormwater drain. He got back into the car and made the long drive to Loman's hardware business in Preston. Just before he got there he pulled into a Mobil self-serve and filled the tank with unleaded. No one saw him also fill the two empty oil containers with the fuel. He filled them to the top: he didn't want fumes building up in them.

Loman ran a big place, taking up one-third of a block at the end of a shopping centre. The N in his name on the sign above the entrance was back to front. The main building was a long, low hardware supermarket fronting onto the street. Behind it was a large storage shed next to a paved area cluttered with do-it-yourself garden shed kits, sample brick walls, and piles of soil and gravel in shades ranging from pinkish-grey to black. A high pineboard fence surrounded the whole place.

In the far corner, well back from the street, was Loman's house, a four-room transportable building resting on wooden blocks. Letterman approached it cautiously, alert for a dog or a nightwatchman, or kids taking short cuts home from the video library. Holding a container of petrol in each hand, he waited for five minutes, watching and listening. He could hear the sound of a television set coming faintly from inside Loman's house. When he was satisfied, Letterman ran doubled-over to the back door. He didn't trip—there was nothing to trip on. The yard surrounding the house looked as if it had been swept to within an inch of its dull life.

Letterman never ate or drank before a job. He felt concentrated, full of nerve endings.

This had to look right. He went from window to window of Loman's house, checking for security alarms. He supposed a man as neat as Loman was, a petty crim like Loman, would have some sort of security fitted, and he found it on every window, a silver strip that would activate an alarm if it were cut.

In other circumstances windows like these were no problem for Letterman. He'd simply pry out the putty surround and move the whole pane aside. But this had to look innocent all the way.

He went around to the front door. It was in darkness and faced a side wall of the storage shed. Putting the litre containers down, he bent to examine the lock. It looked pretty standard. He took out his folder of lock picks and went to work.

There were twenty picks in his kit. He'd got them—and lessons in how to use them—from a crim he'd put in Long Bay five years ago. They were long, flat gunmetal strips with small indentations at various stages and angles along both edges. The kit also contained key blanks, small pry bars and ratchets, but he wouldn't be needing them tonight, only the raking bar. He selected a pick, inserted it into the lock and pushed against the first tumbler pin. Then, inserting the raking bar, he raked the tumbler pin open. He repeated this operation several times, pushing the pick deeper and deeper past the opened tumbler pins.

He reached the end, straightened to ease the strain on his back, and opened the door. He didn't push it fully open but waited and listened. Satisfied that no alarm had gone off, he pushed the door open in stages. Still no alarm sounded. It probably meant that Loman had separate systems for the door and the windows. He'd turn off the door system when he was at home, but generally leave the window system on.

Letterman closed the door. He had stepped straight into a lounge room. The television set wasn't here, though, it was in one of the other rooms.

The bedroom in fact. Through the partly open door he could see Loman stretched out on a monastic-looking single bed, watching a night football game. He wore short pyjamas and a dressing gown. His 'good' leg was horribly scarred. The other was a stump. The plastic leg was on a chair next to the bed. Apparently Loman felt the cold, for a bar heater glowed on a floor rug in the centre of the room.

Letterman didn't waste time. He didn't bother with pointing out Loman's sins to him but ran into the room and stunned him with a heavy blow to the temple. He hit him again.

When he was sure that Loman was fully unconscious he turned off the bar heater. Next he took out his knife and gouged holes in the caps of each petrol container with the sharp, narrow point. He squirted the room with petrol—onto the walls, the wardrobe, the ceiling and the curtains. Apart from the area around the bar heater on the floor, he sprayed high, knowing that the arson squad would be suspicious of intensive burning on the floor or low down on the walls. He made sure the ceiling got plenty. He was relying on it catching early and collapsing on Loman.

Finally he soaked the quilt and dragged a corner of it down to touch the bar heater. Then he turned the heater on and hurriedly stepped back into the doorway. The bed caught at once. When the flames were strong, he tossed the petrol containers onto the bed. They wouldn't last long.

By nine o'clock Letterman was back at his motel arranging an early wake-up call. He showered, packed his bag, and checked his reserves of cash. Thirty thousand dollars—eighteen for Snyder, twelve for expenses. He thought about informing Sydney where he was going but changed his mind. He was his own boss, after all. He didn't have to report in every five minutes like one of their goons. They'd get their report, their pictures, when the job was done.

NINETEEN

Snyder was the last passenger to board the 8.10 am flight to Adelaide on Monday morning. Letterman, stretched out comfortably in first-class with the *Age* for company, saw him come through the door looking like someone who'd always made someone wait. Letterman wanted to slam the heavy, cocksure face. Snyder was a real picture this morning: crisp white overalls again, a chain caught in his throat hair, chunky hippie rings on each hand. For footwear he was wearing dazzling white gym boots. His hair frizzed, catching the light. Letterman, on the other hand, was dressed in a light grey off-the-rack suit from David Jones. He thought, not for the first time, that all kinds flew these days. They didn't make an effort. They flew looking as if they were slopping around the supermarket on a Saturday morning.

At least Snyder didn't make eye contact. 'From now on we don't know each other,' Letterman had told him the day before. He watched as Snyder swaggered through to the economy seats, his cabin baggage knocking the shoulders of passengers seated on the aisle. It was a tough, lightweight aluminium case. His radio gear, Letterman thought.

Breakfast was tinned fruit, toast and watery scrambled eggs. Letterman had the toast and two cups of coffee. It gave him indigestion and he had to ask the stewardess for Quick-eze.

Fifty minutes after take-off they landed at West Beach airport, filed off the plane and across the tarmac. A high wind, laden with hot, oily aviation fumes gusted across the airfield. As usual a couple of uniforms and a plain-clothes man watched them come through the glass doors into the luggage-claim area. Letterman wondered if they had him marked as a cop. He knew he looked like a cop. Despite the last couple of years, he still thought, moved and spoke like a cop.

He collected his bag and reclaimed his automatic from the airline security officer. It was a little .25 loaded with hollow-points. Letterman liked to work close—three or four rounds to the head, the hollow-points breaking up and mashing the brain. He'd had a permit to transport a gun on domestic flights since his days on the force. The airlines never questioned him about it, simply took the gun and gave it back to him at the other end.

Then he went out to the taxi rank. There were signs up advising a passenger-share scheme, but Letterman took one look at the tracksuits and gum-snapping jowls waiting in line and thought fuck that for a joke. He told the driver of the first vacant taxi, 'City bus station,' and got into the back seat. Snyder, he noticed, was getting into a cab with a fluffed-up blonde teenager and her younger sister, baring his teeth at them like a pig at a trough.

'Good flight?'

Letterman looked up. The driver had his head cocked, watching him in the rear-view mirror.

'Just drive,' Letterman said flatly.

The driver opened and closed his mouth, shifted his shoulders around and drove. The traffic was sparse. They reached the bus station in twelve minutes. Letterman paid and got out. Three other taxis rolled up as he closed his door, Snyder's among them. Snyder got out. Letterman saw him wave at the blonde as the taxi departed. He saw the blonde curl her lip at Snyder and go into a huddle with her sister.

Letterman went into the bus station and stood in line at the ticket counter. He looked around while he waited. The linoleum floors were worn and dirty. There were scuff marks on the walls. The lockers were chipped and dented, the plastic seats spotted with cigarette burns. It was nine in the morning and the place was wall to wall human garbage and they were all eating hotdogs. Letterman pictured it: lock the doors, toss in a

Molotov cocktail.

'Where?'

'Vimy Ridge, aisle seat, rear of the bus.'

This seemed to upset the clerk. He stabbed at his keyboard and said, not looking at Letterman: 'Return?'

'Yes.'

The clerk told Letterman the cost. He handled Letterman's money as if it were contaminated. He was a dreary specimen and Letterman wanted this job to be over, wanted to be knocking back oysters and chablis in the sun somewhere.

Letterman was first on the bus. He sat in his seat at the rear, watching the others board. If there was trouble coming, he wanted to be where he could see it. All he saw was Snyder with a paper cup of vinegary chips, a sleepy soldier, a teenager plugged into a Walkman, and half a dozen defeated-looking individuals clutching trashy newspapers and plastic bags.

The bus left at nine-thirty and ran north through farmland. Letterman looked out at the ripening crops and his bleakness grew. He hated it, hated the emptiness, the panicky sheep, the farm kids watching the bus pass with their mouths open. Then he thought he might have to tramp across country like this when he went after Wyatt. He wasn't dressed for it. His mood grew blacker.

The bus drew into Vimy Ridge just before eleven-thirty. It was a rest stop. Everyone filed out of the bus and looked about, blinking and stretching. Letterman was travelling light, only a weekender bag on the rack above his head. He grabbed it and strode across the street and into a café as though he belonged to the place.

The café was cluttered with artifacts from the town's colonial era but Letterman didn't notice that. He sat where he could watch the bus. He ordered coffee, nursing it for the ten minutes the bus was parked in the street. He continued to watch as the bus passengers filed on board again and the bus departed, leaving Snyder waiting there like a clown.

After a while, Snyder began to look at his watch. He picked his nose and peered both ways along the street. Then Letterman saw an old Holden utility pull away from the kerb a few hundred metres away. It had been there when the bus came in. As Letterman watched, the utility drew alongside Snyder. The driver made no sign to Snyder, just watched him. Snyder picked up his bag and approached the utility. He opened the passenger door and leaned in, apparently to talk to the driver. Then he got in and the utility drove away.

Letterman paid at the cash register and asked about accommodation in the town. His blues had vanished. He'd found Wyatt.

TWENTY

'Where we're going there are no shops,' Wyatt said. 'If you need anything—toothpaste, work clothes, whatever—get it now.'

'I could do with some Scotch,' Snyder said.

Wyatt looked at him. Snyder had the red, creased face and heavy belly of a boozer. 'Absolutely no way. I don't care what you do afterwards, the next few days no one drinks.'

'Suit yourself,' Snyder said, making a face at the windscreen. Wyatt was driving painfully slowly through the town. So was everyone else, but that didn't make it any better to Snyder. 'Where we going, anyway?'

'Abandoned farmhouse about half an hour away. We stay there till the job's over.'

'The whole time?'

Wyatt caught a hint of alarm in the voice. He hoped it didn't mean that Snyder got the shakes if he was away from the bottle for too long. 'Ideally, yes. I'll say it again, if you need anything, get it now.'

'Well, I mean, what's this place like? We got beds? Bathroom? Is the power on?'

'That's all taken care of. Army cots, sleeping bags, towels, food, gas stove and lanterns...'

'Who paid for it?'

'I did.'

'You're taking it out of my cut, right?'

'No.'

'Mr Generosity,' Snyder said. He opened the aluminium case. Wyatt had no idea what a jammer looked like, but the radio itself looked impressive. 'All modes,' Snyder went on, 'plus band scanning. I want you to know I paid top dollar for this stuff.'

'You'll be reimbursed.'

'Someone bankrolling this?'

'I am,' Wyatt said.

'From that Melbourne job, right?'

Wyatt stiffened. Loman should have warned him about Snyder. He let it go. There was an agricultural supply place ahead and he slowed the dusty Holden, allowing a farmer to cross the road. The farmer was carrying a small drum of chemical spray in each hand. The drums were heavy, the man bowed down, taking short, laboured steps. He wore khaki work clothes and rubber boots.

'Do you reckon it's true what they say?'

Wyatt had been with Snyder for five minutes and it was five minutes too long. Snyder talked too much, all of it inconsequential. But he made an effort. 'What do they say?'

'It's easier to fuck sheep if you're wearing rubber boots. You just shove the back legs in so they can't get away.'

Wyatt stopped, let the farmer get across, and moved on again. He didn't speak. He saw no reason to speak. He was waiting for Snyder to get his mind around the job.

They reached the edge of the town and Wyatt increased speed. They travelled north for several kilometres and then turned onto a major dirt road. Snyder was sitting forward in his seat. He seemed to be taking a close note of where they were going. 'There are maps at the hideout,' Wyatt said.

Snyder sat back. After a while he said, 'Eddie Loman didn't tell me much.'

'I didn't tell Eddie much.'

Snyder waited. When it was clear that Wyatt wouldn't go on, he said, 'Eddie told me I'd need plastic explosive and radio jamming gear. If I wasn't in the fucking outback, I'd say we were going to do a security van.'

'We are.'

Snyder turned to him. 'Out here?'

'The firm's called Steelgard,' Wyatt said. 'It's a small outfit servicing the local banks, but there's a big construction firm on their books at the moment.'

'Weekly payroll?'

Wyatt nodded.

'Where do we hit?'

'I'm taking you there now.'

Snyder frowned, looking out at the crops and roadside mailboxes. Here and there cypress trees lined farmhouse driveways like green slashes on the dusty landscape. 'I don't like it. It takes too long to cut your way in these days.'

Wyatt explained about the breakdown truck. 'You set your jammer on, we transport the van to the farm, find a way in at our leisure. No panic, no messing about.'

'You can't be serious,' Snyder said. 'The cops will get on the blower and there'll be roadblocks between here and Timbuktu before you know it. I say we go in hard and fast, blow a big hole in it, fuck off straight away.'

It was always like this on a job, Wyatt thought. The soldiers always wanted to be the generals. He said, quietly, coldly, 'You do it my way or not at all. If you want out, tell me now so I can take you back to the bus stop. I'll send you a retainer in a few days time, five thousand dollars. But if I hear you've been sounding your mouth off about me or the job, I'll cancel your ticket.'

'Well, Jesus,' Snyder protested. 'I just thought I was making a valid point. You're telling me we all front up to the roadblocks and hope to Christ the cops don't ask to look in the glovebox? Jesus Christ.'

'We stay inside the area,' Wyatt said. 'After two or three days they'll think we got away at the start and the roadblocks will come down. It's always the same.'

Snyder put his hand on the dashboard as the utility pitched and shuddered over a patch of corrugations in the road. Dust roiled around them, coming through the door seals in choking puffs. 'How will we know when it's safe to leave?'

'One of us scouts around in this,' Wyatt said, patting the steering wheel. 'Just another farm vehicle. If she doesn't come back, we'll know it's not safe.'

'*She*?'

'There's a woman.'

Snyder didn't say anything. He looked at Wyatt, and Wyatt could sense his mind working, but he didn't speak.

A minute later Snyder said, 'Getaway vehicles?'

'There's this ute, a bike, and the truck we use to transport the van.'

'That's the bit I don't like, carting the van around on a breakdown truck. We'll stick out like a sore thumb.'

Wyatt explained about Brava Construction. 'They've had four-wheel drives, low-loaders and earth-moving equipment all over this area for weeks now. People are used to them. We disguise ours with Brava logos and a bit of paint, throw a tarp over the van, and no one will bother us.'

'The guards, the driver?'

'They can stay in the van. If there's a tarp over it they won't see where we're taking them.'

'I tell you one thing,' Snyder said, 'it won't be me who wastes them.'

'No one's wasting anybody. I've got a .38, that's all we need, and I don't intend to use it unless I have to.'

Snyder said nothing. He sat forward in his seat again, taking note of their route. A short time later they came to the Belcowie short cut. Wyatt slowed the utility and turned into it.

'Here?'

Wyatt nodded. He drove for two kilometres and stopped where the road plunged steeply down into a dry creek bed. The road was narrow, loose and shaly.

Snyder leaned forward and grinned. 'Couldn't have picked a better place myself.'

'The truck parks here at the edge of the incline,' Wyatt

explained. 'Our man stands in the road, looking down, scratching his head like he doesn't know if he can make it. The van comes up, sees that it can't get past, and stops. They'll be wary, they always are, but it will *look* genuine enough. They might even wind down the window, offer to help. If they call their headquarters, it won't do them any good. You'll have the radio jammed.'

'What if he backs up and turns around?'

'See those wattles? We hide back there in the ute. As soon as the van is in position we box it in.'

'Local traffic?'

Snyder was asking all the right questions. 'We put up road-closed signs at both ends,' Wyatt said.

Snyder was still leaning forward in his seat. He was a solid form in white and Wyatt could smell Old Spice aftershave on him. There was a series of cracking sounds. Snyder was popping his knuckles.

TWENTY-ONE

Tobin was the last to arrive. They heard him before they saw him. The sky that Monday evening was vast, still and cloudless, carrying clearly the roar and snuffle of the truck as Tobin negotiated the bends and washaways and shifted gear. They stood on the verandah of the farmhouse to watch. Eventually headlights appeared in the distance.

Wyatt walked down the track to open the gate. Behind him, Snyder and Leah talked in low voices. Wyatt had been watching both of them in the hours since his arrival with Snyder. If anything, Snyder seemed to be a little amused by Leah's presence. Wyatt supposed that was better than hostility. Apart from some eye-rolling about the basic food supplies and the house dirt, Snyder was acting pleasant and relaxed. Snyder had done jobs like this before. He knew about being stuck in other people's company. For her part, Leah made an effort to talk to Snyder. She seemed to know that Wyatt had nothing to say to him. But in a snatched moment she'd revealed to Wyatt that she'd never leave her daughter alone with Snyder. If she had a daughter.

Wyatt reached the road gate and waited. When he was sure about the truck, he opened the gate and stepped out into the road, flashing a torch. The truck's headlights flashed back at him.

When Tobin was through the gate, Wyatt closed it and climbed onto the running board below the driver's door.

Tobin grinned at him. 'The others all here?'

'Yes.'

'The woman?'

'Forget about the woman. Tell me about the truck.'

'Pinched it this afternoon. The plates are off a wreck.'

'Tomorrow we paint it. When that's done, we wipe off our prints. After that we wear gloves.'

Tobin shifted into second, muttering aggrievedly, 'You make me feel like this's my first time or something.'

'Your feelings don't interest me. We've each got a job to do. Part of mine is to make sure nothing gets overlooked.'

Tobin scowled. The headlights were picking up the sheds, tankstands and farmhouse by now. Leah and Snyder were on the verandah, shading their eyes.

'Drive into the long shed there on your right,' Wyatt said. 'I'll close the doors behind you.'

He got off the truck and watched. When it was done, he led Tobin across the yard to the house and introduced him to Snyder. Tobin also greeted Leah, throwing his arm around her and grinning. 'We meet again.'

He held her for a beat too long and she grimaced. 'So we do.'

'Yep,' Tobin agreed, still grinning.

The atmosphere got genial after that. They went into the main room of the house, where Wyatt and Leah had laid out the supplies and set up a two-ring camping stove. While Snyder toasted slices of bread on one burner, Leah heated a saucepan of tinned stew on the other. Wyatt got out plastic plates and cutlery and poured mineral water into enamel cups for each of them. Tobin, on the floor with his head on a football he'd taken from his overnight bag, said, 'You giving us poofter drinks?' He grinned at Leah and Snyder, looking for a reaction. Leah smiled at him absent-mindedly. Snyder ignored him. So did Wyatt.

Tobin crossed one ankle over the other and clasped his hands together behind his head. 'What about the sleeping arrangements? Leah, where do you sleep?'

Leah jerked her head towards a door at the end of the room. 'In there.'

'Right, right,' Tobin said. He paused, weighing up his words. 'I suppose women in one room, blokes in another?'

'We each get a room,' Leah said.

'No doubling up, kind of thing?'

'No.'

Wyatt watched all this. Everything about Tobin was loaded. He was saying he liked Leah's looks and might act on it and what did you others intend to do about it?

Separate rooms had been Leah's suggestion. Wyatt could see the sense of it. He realised again how every job was ten per cent work and ninety per cent psychology. If there was any waiting involved, the problem was compounded. He'd always known about the emotional baggage people carried around with them, even when they should have been concentrating on a job. He knew all about hidden grievances, attacks of nerves, insanity and boredom. He didn't want to add sexual jealousy to that. He didn't want Snyder and Tobin smouldering away in the darkness while he shared a room with Leah. And he wasn't worried about Leah. She knew how to handle herself.

'Been a long day,' Tobin said, closing his eyes and stretching. 'Reckon I'll sleep like a baby tonight. Give us a call when tea's ready.'

A small table topped with green linoleum had been left behind at the house. Wyatt dragged it to the centre of the room, set it with the disposable plates and cutlery, and unfolded four canvas and wood director's chairs. Like everything else, the chairs were chosen for easy disposability.

He thought about Snyder. Wyatt never judged whether or not he liked the people he teamed up with. He was interested only in their skills and where the cracks were. Snyder hadn't made a good first impression but once he'd known what the job entailed he'd put his mind to it. Snyder was helping with the domestic work too. That mattered. It meant he knew about teamwork. Somehow Wyatt didn't think they could expect that sort of support from Tobin.

They ate at seven o'clock. No one felt inclined to do anything after that. They sensed the huge darkness and silence outside, while here in the house the lamplight was too meagre to encourage reading, card-playing or talk. They were all asleep by nine o'clock and no one moved until dawn on Tuesday.

They worked hard that day. While Tobin made expert-looking road-closed signs from planks, beaten roofing iron and tins of black and yellow paint, Wyatt helped Snyder paint the break-down-recovery truck pale blue, Brava's colours. The next day Tobin would paint the black bull logo and the words *Brava Construction* on both doors. It was clear that he had a good eye and a steady hand. The truck itself was well-chosen. The tray was long and sturdy. The tailgate was easy to operate, sloping nicely to the ground, and there was a powerful winch system.

At ten o'clock Leah drove down the track in the dusty utility. She wore jeans, shirt and scarf, and was carrying a basket.

'Where's she off to?' Tobin asked.

'Every couple of days she's been going to the short cut to pick wildflowers.'

Tobin stared at Wyatt stolidly, looking for the trick.

'She's checking if the local law ever go down it,' Wyatt explained. 'So far she hasn't seen anyone use it, not even a local farmer, but we have to be sure.'

He watched Tobin to see that he got it. He knew it was important to take pains with Tobin. Tobin had a quick, graceful body, as if he took pleasure in using it, but his mind was plodding. What was worse, he seemed to know it.

'Got you now,' Tobin said.

He went back to slapping paint around. After a while he said, 'She your bird?'

Snyder heard him. He straightened up next to the wheel hubs he was painting and said, 'Leave it, mate.'

'I was only asking.' Tobin went back to his painting. Soon he was whistling a Seekers tune badly.

Wyatt got their minds off it. 'The tarp,' he said. 'I misjudged the size.'

Mustering lost credit, Tobin said, 'Looks like the boss fucked up.'

Wyatt frowned at Snyder, warning him to stay out of it, then turned back to Tobin. 'One of us will have to go and buy another one.'

'There's a hardware in Vimy Ridge,' Tobin said. 'Plus I need toothpaste.'

They watched each other guardedly. Wyatt recognised the signs. Tobin was testing him, asking: do you trust me? If Wyatt said that he couldn't go, the result could be resentment and trouble down the track. Wyatt also knew that he shouldn't go in with Tobin. Tobin would think he was being chaperoned.

They continued to watch each other. Eventually Wyatt nodded. 'Okay. Go in after lunch. Leah will be back by then. I'll give you some money.'

They returned to their painting. Leah reappeared at twelve-thirty and they stopped work to eat sandwiches and drink cups of tea. At one o'clock Tobin changed out of his paint-splashed clothes and drove to Vimy Ridge, $500 of Wyatt's money in his pocket. While Wyatt finished painting the truck, Leah spread maps on the table to familiarise herself with the local roads and Snyder took his big radio to the top of a hill to do a band search.

Tobin returned at four o'clock. He gazed levelly at Wyatt as he got out of the utility, then reached into the back of it and hauled out a tarpaulin. He laid it out on the grass. It was large and new. 'All right?' he said, looking at Wyatt again.

'Perfect.'

They worked until five-thirty. Tobin finished the road-closed signs, then painted a couple of large Brava Construction logos on the tarpaulin. While he did that, the others washed the dirt off the Holden utility and painted it. At five-thirty, when Wyatt announced a halt, Tobin produced his football. He kicked it around with Snyder and Leah until darkness fell. Wyatt appeared to be watching from his chair on the farmhouse verandah, but in fact he was watching only the images in his head, looking at the Steelgard hit from all the angles. Dinner that

night was minestrone soup and spaghetti bolognese. Dessert
was a question and answer session to iron out wrinkles in the
job.

TWENTY-TWO

Letterman hated the country. His suit was wrong, so were his shoes, and he'd had to park several kilometres short of the farm and go the rest of the way on foot. He'd bought the car that morning, soon after Snyder had called him on the radio. It was a clapped-out Valiant that had set him back $1900. He should have spent another hundred and bought some suitable bush gear as well.

But he'd found Wyatt. He climbed through a wire fence and cut back across a paddock to the Valiant. A mistake, he soon realised. The ground was full of traps for the kind of shoes he was wearing. They slipped off the grass tussocks and twisted on concealed stones and rabbit holes. Grass seeds hooked themselves to his socks and trousers. Now that he'd found Wyatt all he wanted to do was go back and wash the dirt off. He badly needed a Quick-eze.

The only accommodation available in Vimy Ridge had been an on-site caravan in the tourist park. Snyder had called him there at one-thirty saying he only had a moment, he was supposed to be doing a band search on his radio.

'Where are you?' Letterman had wanted to know.

'We're camped in this empty farmhouse.'

'How the fuck am I supposed to find you? I told you to come in and get me. I didn't give you that two thousand for nothing.'

'Settle down. One of the others is going in. You can follow him out here.'

'Wyatt?'

'Not Wyatt, a guy called Tobin.' Snyder described Tobin. 'He's picking something up at the hardware. The same ute that picked me up yesterday.'

'I'll find him.'

'I tell you what,' Snyder said, 'it's a sweet job.'

Letterman didn't care about the job. As a concession to Snyder he'd agreed to hit Wyatt when the job was over; what he cared about was how easy Wyatt would be.

'Tell me about Wyatt.'

'He's hard to read. He's all brain and nerve reflexes. On Thursday I wouldn't try announcing myself if I were you. I'd just go in and pop him.'

'What about this Tobin bloke?'

'He's a moron. Wyatt's the only one with a gun. Apart from me.'

There had been a pause. Letterman said, 'Apart from you. How did you get a gun?'

Snyder had been cocky about it. 'Brought it with me. What I do is I strip it and hide the parts with the radio gear so no one knows what it is, then reassemble it later.'

'Very clever. I hope you're not thinking of popping Wyatt. He's strictly mine.'

'It's sort of insurance,' Snyder said. 'You know, in case a certain person decides he might try and get out of paying me what he owes me, kind of thing.'

Letterman had gestured irritably at the wall of his caravan. 'Tell me about the farmhouse. I can't get too close behind this Tobin character.'

'Stop when you come to a tin hut in the corner of a paddock. The farm's off to the right about three or four k's. But we got a deal, you know. You don't pop Wyatt till after the job.'

'Shut up. All I'll be doing is checking out the place. I have to know where to go on Thursday while you're out doing the job.'

'You better time it right Thursday. If Wyatt sees you he'll kill you, no question. If he sees a car shouldn't be there, he could jack it in.'

'Yeah, yeah,' Letterman said. 'Listen, what about the locals?'

'You'll be right,' Snyder said. 'It's the only farmhouse along there.' He'd sniggered a little. 'Tell you what, you could wear one of your suits. If you meet anyone on the road you could tell them you're from the bank. They'll think you've come to repossess and they'll piss off and leave you alone. I like the grey one myself.'

Letterman thought about Snyder's crack now as he stumbled across the paddock. Snyder would be the first to go, no question.

After breaking radio transmission Letterman had left the caravan and gone to look for Tobin. He'd picked up the big hoon at the hardware place, waited while he made a phone call at the post office and shopped at the Four Square supermarket, then settled in a kilometre behind him on the road north from Vimy Ridge. They travelled on the bitumen for several kilometres then turned onto a dirt road. Letterman had hated it. Tobin's utility stirred up thick dust so it was like driving through brown smoke and clouds of it had poured in around the Valiant's pissy door seals. He'd sneezed and cursed and hoped to Christ he didn't have a head-on smash with someone coming from the opposite direction.

Thirty minutes later he'd thought he'd lost Tobin, but then he saw the tin-hut corner. A narrow, pitted track ran off to the right of it. He had parked there and crossed the paddocks in his unsuitable shoes and seen the farmhouse in the distance.

And now he was back at the Valiant, his discomfort forgotten. By Thursday afternoon all this would be over.

TWENTY-THREE

Wyatt normally did nothing on the day before his big heists, but this one was different. He'd never worked with this team before and, knowing what a killer boredom could be, he'd deliberately made the lead-up time short. When Wednesday morning came, he still had plenty of things for them to do.

The most pressing was another question and answer session. He wanted them fresh and rested for that. After breakfast he gathered them at the table with maps, notebooks and cups of tea. Leah, he noticed, looked calm. Snyder's puffy face was creased with recent sleep, but he sounded alert. Tobin had been difficult to wake. He'd held them up for fifteen minutes while he got up and ate a bowl of breakfast cereal, and now he was yawning repeatedly and asking, 'Could you run that past us again?'

Wyatt took them step by step through the job. 'When we leave here tomorrow morning I want the place to look unused in case something goes wrong and we can't come back. I want everything to be buried, prints wiped off every surface, dust spread around. It won't stop a thorough search but there shouldn't be a thorough search if the place *looks* unused. Even so, I don't want them uncovering the little thing that leads back to one of us. I don't want them realising the scale behind this. If all goes well we come back here again for a few days and clean up again when we finally leave.'

Tobin yawned. 'Just a hassle if you ask me.'

Wyatt ignored him. 'At about ten-forty-five we drive the ute and the truck across to the short cut and put up a road-closed sign behind us.'

Snyder's eyes seemed to sink deeper into his fleshy face and frown lines appeared above them. 'Let's hope no one reports it to the local council.'

'It's temporary. We don't want anyone using the short cut while we're getting set up. Leah will be tailing the van on the bike. When she calls to let us know the van's a few minutes away from the turn-off, I'll go back and take the sign down.'

Snyder nodded. 'Meanwhile I monitor the radio in the van?'

'Correct.'

'What about the Belcowie end of the short cut?'

'You and I'll drive along it to check there's no one around. If it's clear, we place the second sign there at the Belcowie end. If someone *is* on the road, we wait. If they look like being a problem, I either call the whole thing off or remove the problem.'

Tobin shot the air with his finger. 'Pow, then chuck them in a ditch.'

Wyatt said nothing. He looked bleakly at Tobin until Tobin started to mutter and shift in his chair. 'Nothing like that,' Wyatt said. 'If some old geezer's feeding his sheep on the road, we tie him up till it's over, nothing else.'

It wasn't scruples or sentiment behind his thinking. There would always be innocent bystanders in the wrong place at the wrong time. What Wyatt cared about was the hue and cry that followed a shooting. The cops were always more energetic when guns were involved.

'So we've cut off the road at both ends,' Snyder said. 'What then?'

'Tobin here parks the truck where the road dips down into the creek and we hide the ute ready to box in the van.'

'You want me to help load?'

'When the time comes. Meanwhile you'll be monitoring the Steelgard frequency ready to jam it.'

'Tricky timing.'

'Leah won't be far behind the van. She warns us in time to take the sign down, and as soon as the van's on the short cut she puts the sign up again.'

'Then I keep watch from that hill opposite,' Leah said. Snyder nodded that he understood. He glanced once at Tobin, twisted his mouth in contempt, looked away again. 'Sounds good.'

'Okay,' Wyatt said. 'Let's run through it again.'

Tobin hadn't kept still all this time. He continued to yawn at intervals and twist restlessly in his chair. He wore brief shorts and a singlet, so he seemed to be a mass of flesh, all of it bored. 'Ah, pack it in. We'll be right.'

Wyatt leaned forward. He kept his voice low. 'If you fuck up tomorrow, I'll kill you.'

Tobin threw up his arms and rolled his eyes. 'Fucking charming. You others hear that?'

'Can it, Tobin,' Snyder said.

Tobin turned to Leah. He leaned an elbow on the table and rested his head on his hand. 'What about you? Want to come outside, leave the boys to do the thinking?'

Leah smiled coldly at him. 'Want to stay here like a good boy and listen to the men? You might learn something.'

Tobin flushed and jerked back. 'Yeah, well I know all about you, you moll.'

No one moved, waiting to see what else Tobin would do. Leah stared at him neutrally. Snyder tipped back in his chair, watching like someone interested but not involved. Wyatt held himself ready to smack Tobin down if it came to that.

When nothing happened, he said patiently, 'Let's run through it again. This time you each tell me.'

One by one they described their part in the heist. Tobin surprised them by summarising his role exactly and leaving nothing out. But he didn't look at anyone, and his tone was choppy and contemptuous.

When they were all finished Wyatt said, 'Now the period after the job.'

He was looking at Tobin. He expected trouble from him. He didn't think Tobin would have the patience to wait around after the job. But Tobin was unusually compliant, swirling his cup, looking at the tea-leaves.

Wyatt explained it anyway. 'Time and distance are against us. When the van goes off the air, and it doesn't show in Belcowie, the whole of the mid-north will go on alert. Patrols, roadblocks, you name it. We'd never make it.'

He paused, watching Tobin. Tobin's face was changing expression rapidly, as though he were having a conversation with himself. Wyatt went on. 'We stay here until it's safe to leave. I don't want anything to show from the air, and we don't go outside unless it's safe to do so. We post a lookout, four-hour shifts around the clock. I doubt if there'll be a ground search here—it's off the beaten track and with any luck they'll think the van's been driven interstate or something—but if there is, we'll see them coming in time to get out the back way.'

He stopped, looking at Snyder. Snyder had been listening, but it had been polite, as if he were going through the motions. Now he seemed to sharpen. 'Plan B?' he said.

Wyatt knew what he meant. 'If something goes wrong, if I'm recognised or Leah spots cops in the area, we abandon. We don't come back here at all.'

Snyder gave him a complicated look. 'That would be a pisser. What about the van? What if it changes route?'

'We'll soon know if it does.'

'And?'

'We abandon.'

Snyder shrugged fatalistically. Wyatt looked at Tobin. Tobin had his hands behind his head. He continued to look bored, as if none of this had anything to do with him.

'You taking this in?'

'Fuckin' A,' Tobin said. 'If I fuck up, you'll waste me.'

He looked at the ceiling and began to whistle silently.

The danger signals were clear. But Wyatt had covered everything, so he closed the meeting. It was almost midday. They had lunch, then spent the afternoon taking care of the finishing touches. While Tobin painted the Brava logo on both vehicles,

Wyatt and Snyder fitted and tested the radios and the radio jammer, and Leah collected and buried rubbish and cleaned the brushes. Tobin was silent and aggrieved for most of the afternoon but at five-thirty he got out his football again. This time they all kicked it around.

TWENTY-FOUR

'The condemned man ate a hearty breakfast,' Leah said.

Wyatt felt her kick him under the table. He looked up. She was watching Tobin eat. So was Snyder. Like Wyatt, they had eaten small bowls of porridge and were sipping strong coffee, not having the stomach for anything else, but Tobin had eaten two bowls of porridge and was now attacking a mound of scrambled eggs and bacon. They heard the slush of the food in his mouth and gullet. They heard him swallow. And he was eating rapidly, as if this were his last meal.

Wyatt returned her smile abstractedly and looked away again. Now that they were ready to go, he felt concentrated and still. He'd eaten little, not from nerves but because food didn't interest him just then. It would be different afterwards. Afterwards he would be high on adrenalin and in need of food to bring himself down. He would also need Leah. But he didn't think about any of that. At this stage he had no emotional stake in what they were doing or what the results would be. He was waiting like a piece of machinery that won't activate itself until after other machinery has been set in motion.

He got up and left the room. He stood on the verandah for a while, drinking coffee, looking out across the valley. Visibility was good, the sky clear and windless. There was no indication of storms or other atmospheric conditions that might interfere with radio transmissions. A sparrowhawk floated on the air currents some distance away. A fieldmouse, he thought. Maybe a quail or plover chick. As he watched, the bird seemed to close up with a snap and plunge earthwards, coming out of the dive at the last second with the creature in its talons.

Leah joined him, trailing her fingers briefly across the seat of his pants before standing there dreamily, both hands clutching her cup of coffee. 'The waiting game,' she said.

It was always like this before a job. Wyatt had never worked with anyone who hadn't got jumpy and needed to talk. Normally he kept out of their way and if that wasn't possible, he closed his eyes until they shut up and left him alone. Something told him now not to do that to Leah. For the sake of her peace of mind, he said the sort of thing he knew people expected to hear. 'Yep, always the same.'

In fact he had no feelings one way or the other about waiting. He knew that waiting rattled other people, and he knew why, but not because he'd experienced it himself. It was the machine part of him again.

'You must be used to it by now,' Leah went on.

'It doesn't do to get too relaxed,' he replied, playing the part. 'You have to stay alert.'

She nodded as if he'd expressed an essential truth. She jerked her head. 'It's going to be hard spending time here with those two afterwards. It's going to be like an anti-climax.'

Wyatt nodded. She was talking sense now, not platitudes. A lot of jobs go sour if waiting is involved *after* the hit has been made. That's when the bickering and dissension start. The hotheads decide they deserve a bigger cut and have to be placated. The cowboys want to take off and start spending their money and have to be stopped before they get caught and lead the cops back to you. It came down to psychology.

'It's the way they watch me,' Leah continued. 'They'll be high after this. We'll have to watch our backs.'

'If there's any bullshit,' Wyatt said, 'we hit hard and fast.'

At nine o'clock they changed into brown overalls and Wyatt directed them in a detailed clean-up of the farm. They buried tins, paper and food scraps in the pit, then raked it over and disguised it with stones and rusty fencing wire and strainers. The fold-up chairs, sleeping bags, camping stove and personal belongings were stacked in the tray of the utility, ready to be taken out and used again when and if they did return. They put on latex gloves then and wiped their prints off every surface in the house. They spread a fine layer of dirt over the floors. Finally Wyatt distributed the balaclavas and hand-held radios. Snyder already had his radio and jammer tuned to the Steelgard frequency. The signal was clear. The driver was reporting in every five minutes and he was on schedule.

Wyatt sent Leah off first. She had thirty minutes to reach Vimy Ridge on the Suzuki and pick up the Steelgard van. Then he and Snyder left in the Holden utility, followed by Tobin in the truck. Twenty minutes later they turned onto the short cut and Snyder placed a road-closed sign across the entrance. Tobin pulled over into the grass at the side of the track near the creek bed, letting Wyatt and Snyder edge past him. They saw no one on the track, and at the junction near Belcowie, Snyder put the second sign in place. Then they drove back to Tobin. When the utility was concealed, Tobin blocked the road with the truck. The rear was in the centre of the track. All they had to do when they had the van blocked was drop the ramp and winch it aboard.

The three men settled down to wait. Every five minutes the Steelgard van announced its position and progress. Wyatt checked his watch: eleven twenty-five. As if on cue, the radio came to life again: 'Steelgard One.'

'Go ahead, Steelgard One.'

'Leaving Vimy Ridge. On schedule. ETA Belcowie approximately twelve midday.'

'Roger, Steelgard One.'

Tobin sniggered and adjusted his reflective orange lenses. 'Just like the movies.'

'Go and wait in the truck,' Wyatt said. 'Any last minute questions?'

'Not me, mate.'

Wyatt settled back in his seat. Leah would be following the van now. He calculated that they had about twenty minutes before the van reached the short cut. He didn't need to look at his watch to know. When he was operating at this level of concentration, he knew how to judge time.

The radio crackled. It was Leah. She didn't use names; she simply said, 'Move.'

'Moving,' Wyatt said.

He got out of the utility and jogged back along the track to the first road sign. He hid it where Leah could find it in the long grass of the roadside ditch then returned to the utility. Five minutes.

'So,' Snyder said.

Wyatt almost frowned. Here it was again, the need to make an effort to keep someone happy or calm. But he usually did make the effort. He knew people found him solid and reassuring. He was impersonal, so nothing about him threatened them. When he was wasn't working he made no particular effort to get along with people, and that was the time he liked best.

'Not long now,' he said. He couldn't think of anything else to say.

'Thought what you're going to do with your cut?'

'Holiday,' Wyatt said. 'Buy a new place.'

'I heard you had to dump everything after that job in Melbourne.'

Wyatt's senses tingled. There it was again, oblique references to his last job. 'It happens.'

'Me, I'm investing in real estate,' Snyder said. 'The market's low at the moment. Good time to buy.'

'Yes,' Wyatt said.

Something about Snyder bothered Wyatt. It wasn't what Snyder was saying, it was something about his attitude. He seemed to be playing a game—almost, Wyatt thought, as if he's going through the motions, as if he's not listening. Snyder's face was giving nothing away, but something was there.

He pushed that away. He sensed it was time for Leah's signal. He began to prepare himself for it.

When her voice did come over the radio it was breathless and panicky.

'Something's wrong. It didn't stop. It's gone on past the turn-off.'

TWENTY-FIVE

'We abandon,' Wyatt said.

He looked at them in turn. Leah had just ridden up on the Suzuki. She looked bleak, defeated, scraping her palms down her cheeks as if to rid herself of tiredness. Tobin paced next to the truck, landing occasional kicks on the rear tyres. Only Snyder was still, staring at Wyatt, his eyes hard and suspicious.

'All that time and effort,' Leah said.

'It happens.'

'We could try next week.'

'No chance,' Wyatt said. 'They've changed the route.'

'But why?'

'I can think of a lot of reasons. It's routine; the driver wanted a change of scenery; something's made them suspicious.'

Snyder sharpened at that. 'Suspicious?'

'It doesn't matter what the reason is,' Wyatt said. And it didn't, to him—not when saving their necks was more important than dwelling on what went wrong or what might have been. The analysis could come later. 'We have to clear out, the sooner the better.'

'Like where?'

'Wherever you like. Come on, let's get moving, or someone's going to wonder about the road signs and extra traffic.'

The radio crackled again. 'Steelgard One.'

'Go ahead, Steelgard One.'

'On schedule, nothing to report, ETA Belcowie unchanged.'

The exchange was brief and sudden, and for a few moments it froze them to the spot. Wyatt stirred first. 'We split up. Snyder, take the bike. Catch the first plane home. Leah, you come with me. Tobin, you take the truck. Dump it somewhere and catch a train or a bus home.'

Snyder stepped forward. 'Hang on, I don't like this.'

Wyatt tensed. 'What don't you like?'

'Splitting up, pissing off. I don't think we should leave until we know what went wrong.'

'Leave me out of this,' Tobin said. He climbed quickly into the cabin, started the engine and eased the big truck across the dry creek bed. Soon he was a dust cloud receding from them.

Wyatt turned his attention to Snyder again. He wondered if Snyder had lost all his commonsense. He looked at the heavy, acned face, trying to read behind it. Snyder looked confused and anxious.

'Plus,' Snyder went on, 'I'm out of pocket on this bloody deal.'

This was more like it. 'You'll all get a kill fee,' Wyatt said.

'How much?'

'Five thousand on top of your expenses.'

Snyder held out his hand. 'Let's see it first.'

'Don't be stupid. You'll get it later.'

'Not good enough,' Snyder said, and he reached into the pocket of his overalls and pulled out a small automatic pistol. The sky above them was vastly blue and still, so the sound of Snyder jacking a round into the firing chamber was like a twig snapping. No one moved. Then, as Wyatt was about to speak, the Steelgard van reported in again. *On schedule. Nothing to report.*

Snyder gestured with his pistol. He looked flushed and edgy, as if rolling with a plan that might come unstuck at any minute.

Wyatt stood, his body loose, ready to take Snyder. He was starting to read the other man. Snyder had been expecting a hundred grand. Compared to that, a fee of five thousand dollars was peanuts. Killing Wyatt was the only thing that would satisfy him now. 'Put the gun away, Snyder,' he said. 'Let's talk this over.'

Snyder shook his head. 'Uh, uh. Chuck me your gun before we do anything. Barrel first, that's right, now drop it on the ground and kick it out of the way.'

Wyatt did as he was told. Snyder was too far back for him to try anything.

'You'll regret this,' Leah said.

Snyder's agitation was getting more pronounced. He seemed to be running against the clock. 'Shut up. Help Wyatt load the bike.'

'There's no need for this,' she said, dropping the tailboard of the utility. 'We'll pay you when we get to my place. We don't want to hang around here.'

Snyder grinned again, a nervy grimace as he stepped from one foot to the other. 'Bugger your place.'

Wyatt had clicked the Suzuki into neutral with his foot and was wheeling it toward the rear of the Holden. He stopped, looking hard at Snyder, thinking it through. If Snyder intended to kill them, it made sense to do it at the farmhouse where their bodies might never be found.

Snyder swung around on him, the gun arm taut and quivering. 'Who told you to stop? Load the fucking bike.'

Leah chose that moment to reach into the tray of the utility, haul out one of the folding chairs, and toss it at Snyder. It flew on its side, spinning end to end, and hit Snyder low, the edge of the frame mashing him between the legs. He doubled over, his knees together, and cried out. He had the automatic raised to fire blindly at them when Wyatt, ducking low, pushed the bike at him. Snyder went down onto his hip, pinned by the bike. Wyatt rushed him. He stamped on Snyder's fingers, prised the pistol out of his hands and shot him twice in the head.

Then he backed away and watched Snyder die. He was not breathing heavily or showing other signs of heightened emotion. If anything, he was frowning, as though some minor hitch was bugging him.

TWENTY-SIX

Then he turned around. 'Leah,' he said.

He made the word sharp and clear, to get her attention. She was looking down, paralysed, at Snyder. People see killings on films all the time, but it never prepares them for the real thing. The real thing—even one man punching another—is shocking: the sound, the suddenness and emptiness. Wyatt didn't want her to slide into depression again. He had to snap her out of it. '*Leah*.'

She continued to look down at the body. 'Just like that.'

'He was going to kill us.'

She gestured helplessly. 'Everything's changed.'

'Nothing's changed. We bury him first, that's all.'

'Where?'

'The farm, fuck it. We can't leave him out here, and we can't risk carting him around.'

At that moment, the Steelgard driver called in again, gabbling a little as if relieved to be near the end of the line. *ETA Belcowie, fifteen minutes.*

Wyatt turned the radio off. He had to get Leah moving, get her thinking about survival, not emotions. 'Grab his feet.'

'His feet?'

'Help me put him in the ute. Grab his feet.'

He thought she might lose it again. Her face was strained. But then she bent down, grabbed Snyder's feet, and they lifted together. It brought the colour back to her face. They tumbled Snyder into the tray and Wyatt unzipped the sleeping bags and covered the body. Then he hauled the bike onto its wheels. Fuel had sloshed onto the road and the engine was smeared with dirt but it started immediately, smoking a little before it cleared.

'You go on ahead,' he said, 'while I pick up the road signs. Call me on the radio if you see anything that shouldn't be there.'

Her face changed again. She seemed to recoil from him. 'No thanks, I'm going home. I don't need this.'

She put on her helmet and swung her leg over the bike. Wyatt didn't say anything. He watched her go. He put her out of his mind then and got into the utility and drove to the far end of the short cut. He found the road sign where Tobin had tossed it into the grass. He loaded it, turned around and doubled back.

This was automatic, taking care of the loose ends. He did it calmly and systematically. Behind it he was thinking hard. Steelgard's route change bothered him. So did the business with Snyder. He turned on the radio again.

The drive back to the turn-off took him five minutes. He got out, collected the other road sign, and tossed it into the back of the utility. Seven minutes. He turned left onto the main road and accelerated toward the tin-hut corner. Eleven minutes. He felt uneasy, then realised why. There should have been something on the radio by now.

That's when the voice erupted, tinged with worry. 'Steelgard One, this is Goyder Base, are you receiving me, over?'

Wyatt leaned forward, listening, imagining the dispatcher hunched over the transmitter dials.

'Steelgard One, this is Goyder Base, your position please, over.'

There was real concern in the voice now. Wyatt drove on, picturing it from their end. Goyder Base would continue to call the van, but by now they would also be talking to the Brava pay officer in Belcowie. They would spend a couple of minutes debating whether or not it was too soon to call the cops. The cops would spend a few minutes asking questions before deciding to send a car out. It would take the cops thirty minutes to arrive and begin the search.

Perhaps forty minutes altogether. Leah would be okay. She'd be long gone by then. Wyatt slowed, turned the utility around and retraced the van's route past the turn-off. He took it slowly. He knew how deceptive an open country road could be. There are always haystacks, fire-water tanks, clumps of trees, ditches and roadside farm buildings along them. He slowed to a walking pace whenever he passed one of these, accelerating again when he saw there was no Steelgard van sheltering there.

The most likely place was a side road. He stopped and got out at the first two. There were tracks, but not the tracks he remembered seeing left by the van on the short cut a week ago.

He found the answer at the third side road. A detour sign had been tossed into the grass. The dirt was powdery, registering clearly the tyre tracks of a heavy vehicle. Wyatt remembered from the maps that this track came out four kilometres south of Belcowie.

He went in. He didn't find the van, but he found where it had stopped. Found the fat driver sprawled in the ditch, the back of his head shot away.

TWENTY-SEVEN

Trigg hadn't been one hundred per cent sure that Tub Venables would do it. He knew Venables wouldn't take his regular route, not after he'd learnt that a hold up team was waiting for him, but what if the fat driver chickened out and went the long way around to Belcowie?

He'd been wondering what he'd do if that happened when Happy's voice crackled on the two-way radio. 'Boss? He just turned in.'

Trigg sat up, peering down the long bonnet of an XJ6 he'd been trying to sell for the past six months. Probably it wasn't a good idea bringing an XJ6 onto a road like this, but he hated the thought of driving some tin can. 'Okay. Put the sign up and follow him in.'

Trigg reached into the back seat, slipped a .303 rifle from its zippered bag, and got out to wait. He heard the Steelgard van, then saw it, pitching on the rough track like a ship in mountainous seas.

Venables stopped the van a few metres short of the big car and stepped out. He looked at the rifle, then at Trigg, his eyes bulging a little, the lines on his face loose and deep. For the moment, they were alone. There were only the empty paddocks and distant razorback hills.

Trigg nodded his head at the rear compartment of the security van. 'Is he out?'

Venables's face knitted in worry. 'He's on the floor. You sure he's okay?'

'He'll have a headache when he wakes up. Apart from that, he'll be fine.'

They heard footsteps thudding in the grass at the edge of

the track. Happy appeared, his gloomy face showing the strain. 'Okay?' Trigg asked.

'Yep.'

'Good,' Trigg said. Then, to Venables: 'It's time you called in again.'

Venables's prominent eyes were watery and troubled. He reached into the cab of the Steelgard van for the radio handset. His voice rasping a little, he reported to the base in Goyder: 'Steelgard One; nothing to report; ETA Belcowie fifteen minutes.'

'Good,' Trigg said again, and he tucked the front sight of the .303 under Tub Venables's chin and pulled the trigger. There was a spurt of blood and bone chips and Venables seemed to spring up and back and smack to the ground. For several seconds afterwards, tremors passed through his arms and legs.

'Dump him in the ditch,' Trigg said. 'We don't want him found yet.'

He wasn't worried about a ballistics test. The slug would have gone right through Venables's head. He wasn't particularly worried about the rifle. A drifter had given it to him five years ago in part payment for a clapped out VW. There was no paperwork linking him to it, and he didn't intend to hang onto it.

He watched Happy haul the body off the road. Then he got into the XJ6 and Happy into the Steelgard van and they drove along the track for three minutes. Tobin was waiting for them next to an earthen bank thick with tall Scotch thistles and reeds that screened them from traffic passing along the Belcowie road a short distance away. Tobin had just arrived. He was dropping the ramp at the back of the breakdown truck. No one spoke until Happy, guided by Tobin's hand signals, had the van aboard the truck.

'Where's the driver?' Tobin asked.

Trigg stared moodily into the distance. 'He couldn't make it. Help Hap get the tarp over the van.'

While they were doing that, Trigg went back to move the first sign. The signs would attract attention when the panic started, and he didn't want Venables found just yet. He hid the sign in the grass and drove back to the truck. The van was completely concealed now, the tarpaulin covering it on all sides. The paint job, the logo on the side—Wyatt's team had done a good job.

They pulled out. Trigg went first, to drag the second sign into the grass, and Tobin and Happy followed in the truck. At the intersection they turned left, away from Belcowie. There was no traffic.

Trigg led all the way, keeping in radio contact with the others. He didn't think there would be a roadblock this soon, not until the cops had searched and scratched their heads for a while, but he wasn't taking any chances. If there was a block, he'd have time to warn the others. He imagined the confusion when the police did find something. When they found Tub Venables but no van, they might be inclined to blame the guard. If they found the hideout, found Wyatt and the woman and the other man, they'd think they had it solved.

There were no roadblocks. In fact, the bogus Brava truck and its cargo were locked in the long panel-beating shed at the rear of Trigg Motors in Goyder two minutes before the first Goyder patrol car had even left the city.

TWENTY-EIGHT

The blood had begun to coagulate and flies were gathering but the body was still warm. The fat driver looked less fat now that he'd been shot and dumped in a roadside ditch. Wyatt wondered why Venables had taken this route, why he had stopped, why he had left the van.

He examined the tracks. Apart from Venables's heel scrapes in the powdery dirt, there were two sets of tyre tracks—the Steelgard van and a narrower set belonging to a car. Both had stopped here, something had happened, and both had gone on again.

Maybe they wouldn't be far ahead. Wyatt started the utility again and put his foot down, the elderly suspension complaining, the sump smacking against the hard-baked ruts in the road.

He got to the end and stopped. The main road to Belcowie was empty. There was only a shot-up road sign warning of the T-intersection and indicating that Belcowie was four kilometres to the north, Goyder seventy to the south. He got out to see if he could read the tracks. There weren't any. Gravel had been spread around the junction, too coarse to register tyre tracks. But something had been dragged across it recently. Wyatt followed the scrape mark into the thick grass leading to a strainer post in the fence on the left-hand corner paddock. Someone had dumped a road-closed sign there. It was cruder than the ones Leah and Snyder had made.

He returned to the utility. The intersection was on a slight rise. He could see Belcowie clearly, the wheat silos glowing white, sunlight flashing on windscreens and rooftops.

He turned his head the other way. South, he thought. That's where they'll be.

He was about to head after them when something about the scope and intensity of the flashing windscreens made him pause and get out the field-glasses. At one point between the intersection and Belcowie the road curved broadly to skirt a large limestone reef. Within a few seconds he saw what the fuss was about. Four of the Brava Landcruisers were pushing fast out of the town. He guessed there would be more like it setting out from the other end of the town. Jorge was sending out search parties. His men were volatile and wanted their wages.

Wyatt spun the utility around, cursing himself. He should have thought of that, should have realised Steelgard wouldn't be alone in wondering where the money had got to.

He threw the Holden into the bends and over the bone-jarring ruts and holes of the track. He had to get out and onto a main road before they squeezed him from both ends. If they saw him they'd know the utility wasn't one of theirs. If they found Venables's body, they'd assume he'd done it. They'd call each other on their CB radios and box him in. They'd call the cops. If they caught him they wouldn't find any money but they'd find Snyder under the sleeping bags and plenty of evidence of a planned job. They'd find enough to put him away for life.

For a few seconds, when the track was flat and smooth, Wyatt risked giving his attention to Snyder's fancy radio. It was turned low, still tuned to the monotonous Steelgard dispatcher. He switched to the CB band and tuned it to the channel used by Brava.

Excited voices erupted in Spanish and English. They knew each other, so no one was bothering with formalities.

'Jorge said no heroics, wait for the police.'

'Fuck that. By the time the cops get here the bastards'll be long gone.'

'Maybe is no been robbed. Maybe is lost, is no more gasoline in the tank. Maybe the radio he is broken.'

'So how come there's no sign of the van? How come he changed his route?'

'Yeah.'

'Yeah.'

Then a voice said, 'The chopper will find them.'

Wyatt went cold, remembering the gasfields helicopter. Several times a month it flew geologists and engineers down to confer with Jorge. If this was one of those times, it was probably already in the air, starting a sweep of the area.

'Plus there's an air ambulance coming down from Port Augusta,' the voice continued.

'No worries, then,' said another voice. 'We'll find the bastards in no time.'

Half a dozen other voices agreed.

Wyatt pushed even harder along the track, feeling the old chassis bottom out on the outcrops of stone. If they spotted him from the air, he was finished. They'd guide the land party in until all his exits were closed. His only chance was to get to the farm, get the Holden into one of the sheds, then escape on foot across country.

Meanwhile Leah deserved a better chance. He called her. There was no answer. Perhaps she couldn't hear him. She'd be kilometres away by now, probably well out of radio range. He called again, waited, and called a third time.

He didn't try again. He felt the strain of listening, the strain of driving one-handed along the tortuous track.

For just a few moments then he had a clear view of the Vimy Ridge road. A lone Brava Landcruiser had braked beyond the turn-off and was backing up to it.

There was only one way out of this. Wyatt pulled up next to Venables's body and turned off the engine. Ejecting the cartridges from Snyder's pistol and using the butt as a hammer, he destroyed the big radio. Then he opened both doors wide and shot the front tyres with his own gun. He threw Snyder's gun into the grass. He was still wearing latex gloves so he wasn't worried about prints.

Part of the fence line along this section of the track was a stone wall built by shepherds in the nineteenth century. Flat stones the size of frying pans had been stacked chest-high for several hundred metres. Here and there parts of the wall had collapsed. Wyatt vaulted through a gap and got ready to wait, disturbing a tiny brown lizard. The lizard flicked away in the space of an eye blink.

It wasn't much of a trap but it had the element of confusion—a stationary vehicle, both its doors open; a dead man in the grass; the fake Brava paint job; the empty road under the spooked sky.

They weren't taking any chances. He watched as the Landcruiser approached slowly and stopped fifty metres short of the Holden utility. There were two men aboard. They didn't get out but waited there, the engine running. One of them was calling on the CB radio. Wyatt recognised him. It was Carlos.

Half a minute later, Carlos got out and cautiously walked towards the body and the stranded utility. He was carrying a heavy tyre iron. There were guns in the Brava camp, but they were kept under lock and key in Jorge's safe.

Wyatt watched Carlos circle the Holden, look around apprehensively, his eyes passing over Wyatt's hiding place, and crouch next to the dead driver. He seemed to recoil in shock then, stepping back from the body and signalling urgently to the other man.

Wyatt waited until they were both standing there in the road, looking down at the glistening skull, their guard down. He vaulted the wall again and took them at a run. They heard him and turned around. Slowly their hands went up.

Carlos spoke first. 'They will catch you, my friend.' He gestured at the sky and spun the tip of his forefinger. 'The aeroplane, he comes now.'

The other man had red curly hair and a sneering mouth. 'Mad bastard.'

'Shut up. The keys,' Wyatt said.

'In the ignition.'

Wyatt nodded and began to back away from them.

'Where's the fucking money?'

Wyatt ignored them. When he was a few metres away from the Landcruiser he turned and sprinted the rest of the way. A minute later he was on the Vimy Ridge road again, just another mad Latin adding to the confusion on the ground.

TWENTY-NINE

They were going crazy in the Brava camp. Eight of the pale blue Landcruisers with the bull logo passed Wyatt in the first five minutes. They were being driven carelessly and fast—but at least they weren't stopping him to ask who he was. He drove slouched over the wheel, lifting a finger as they passed—a custom which the Brava crews had adopted from the locals. It helped that he was wearing the sunglasses and bright orange baseball cap left by Carlos on the driver's seat, but what helped most was the high spirits in the Brava camp. Wyatt was driving a Brava vehicle so they assumed he was caught up in it too.

But Wyatt knew that the disguise was only good for another few minutes and wasn't good enough to get him past a road-block. He'd have to go to ground at the farm.

He was thinking it through when headlights on an oncoming car flashed at him and a blue light started to pulse on its roof. A policeman stepped into the middle of the road with his hand raised, waving him down. Wyatt got ready. Slowing the Landcruiser, he slipped his .38 out of his belt and onto the seat beside him, covering it with his hand.

He pulled up twenty metres short of the police car and left the engine running. He was about to put his foot down but something told him to think twice about it. The cop's expression was wrong. He wasn't wary. He wasn't expecting trouble. If anything he was angry. Wyatt wound down his window. 'G'day,' he said.

'Don't g'day me. Do you arseholes know what you're doing?'

'Sorry?'

'One of you blokes has already rolled over. I nearly smashed head-on with another one. You're buggerising around inside an official crime scene. Piss off before I lock you up.'

'Sorry, just trying to help.'

'Go and do it somewhere else. If you see any of your mates, pass it on—anyone found farting around gets the book thrown at him.'

'Sure, no worries,' Wyatt said. He lifted his foot off the clutch, nodded at the cop and pulled away.

'Bloody cowboys,' he heard the cop say.

Wyatt watched him in the rear-view mirror. He saw him shake his head, climb into the patrol car, and pull away fast, spinning tyres in the roadside gravel. The blue light faded in the dust like a special effect.

No one else bothered Wyatt after that. He came to the tin-hut corner a few minutes later, paused for half a minute, and bounced his way towards the farm gate. He saw dust in the distance, from all the excitement, but no vehicles were close enough to spot him. The helicopter was several kilometres away, sweeping back and forth across the valley. Eventually it would pass over the farmhouse, but now it was concentrating the search around the turn-off.

Wyatt first began to doubt Leah when he got to the implement shed and found the Suzuki there. The door was open, the bike on its stand in the corner. The doubts weren't specific—he just wanted to know what she was doing there.

He drove the Brava Landcruiser into the musty interior, switched off, and got out, holding the .38 loose at his side. He didn't go into the house immediately. He closed the massive shed door then waited outside it for a few minutes, testing the air, giving Leah a chance to come out of the house. The helicopter was now a few degrees left of where it had been. It was hovering, beginning to settle on the ground. They'd found Venables.

Wyatt turned and crossed the yard. He needed only a minute to see that the house was empty. He searched the sheds. Nothing. He told himself that she'd got spooked by the helicopter and made a run for it.

But it didn't feel right. And when he found faint tyre marks on the track behind the property, the doubts set in and wouldn't go away.

He went to the head of the driveway to sweep the valley with his field-glasses. The helicopter had just completed a sweep near the tin-hut corner. Beneath it the roads were dust-clogged.

The ground party was congregating. They'd be at the farmhouse soon, wondering if this was where the murderers had got to.

THIRTY

Wyatt wheeled the Suzuki out of the shed. He could hear the flat *whump whump* of the helicopter now. He shook the bike—fuel sloshed in the tank. He climbed on, pushed hard on the kick-start and accelerated across the yard. A minute later he was on the track leading back into the ranges behind the farmhouse.

He had advantages on a bike. He hoped they'd be enough. It was faster than walking and he could go where a car couldn't go. The cops would be blocking the roads but they couldn't throw a cordon over paddocks and creeks. That was what Wyatt was relying on. That and speed.

He looked back over his shoulder briefly, almost losing the bike in an erosion channel. The helicopter was apparently closing in on the farm. Wyatt hoped they'd concentrate on the house and sheds and not the hills behind it just yet. He was a small shape, dressed in dull khaki overalls, but he knew it was movement that attracts attention from the air, not shape, size or colour.

He righted the bike, his eyes darting from the ground surface under his wheels to the shape of the land ahead. He didn't want to tie himself to the track if he could save time by heading across country. Using his eyes and his mental map, he began to plot his route out of the hills. He knew what to avoid—the dry creekbeds with their treacherous sand; stone reefs like stakes embedded in the wind-blasted hillsides; foxholes and rusty fencing wire in the long grass.

In other circumstances he might have enjoyed his flight across the forgotten back country. They said land like this was bland—blindness, Wyatt thought, taking in the purples and greens, the tortured shapes. The sun was mild on his back.

The spring wildflowers were out and the sky was cloudless. He risked another glance over his shoulder. The farmhouse and sheds were out of view. There was no helicopter yet.

But the reversals of the past hour wouldn't let him alone. He thought about Leah's STD call to her contact, her trips away from the farm. Snyder puzzled him. Snyder had been too keen to go back to the farmhouse. He felt more certain about Tobin. Given that the other aspects of the plan had been duplicated, it was reasonable to suppose that Tobin had been used to shift the van. And it was Leah who'd brought Tobin into the team.

He'd find her. He'd find both of them.

He began to pick a way out of the worst of the stone reefs and hidden gullies. Before him lay undulating farmland. It was fenced, immense paddocks of grassy slopes dotted with ancient gum trees. Sheep had spread across one end of the closest paddock, several hundred of them grazing head down in the long grass. He opened a gate, closed it behind him and set out across the paddock, mindful that snarls of fencing wire might be caught in the grass. There was a gravel road at the far end of the paddock. He intended to travel along it for a few kilometres then cut across country again.

Something passed across the sun behind him. It threw a shadow that was gone as suddenly as it was there. Wyatt didn't look back or increase speed. He changed direction slightly. A few seconds later he was wobbling in low gear at the leading edge of the sheep.

Wyatt had built his life on blending in so he wouldn't be noticed. It was automatic. Now he was doing it again. He steered in and around the sheep, stopping occasionally, waving an arm. He'd never done anything like this before. He didn't know anything about sheep. But they seemed to be doing the right thing. They were fat, their bellies full, and they moved hurriedly a short distance and appeared to forget about him again, yet bit by bit they were bunching up. Now and then some of them streamed away from the mob, wild-eyed and mindless, but he had no trouble heading them off. He hoped it looked right from the air. He lacked one essential prop, a dog, but he hoped he looked as though he belonged here.

Then he did something he'd seen a farmer do a few weeks earlier, when he was pipe-laying north of Belcowie. Standing the bike on its stand, he charged into the mob, wrestled a sheep to the ground, and leaned down to examine its hindquarters.

When the Brava helicopter stopped circling, dropping to just above the ground fifty metres away, the pilot and passengers saw a farmer start in surprise, a sheep propped butt down against his knees. The surprise changed to anger. He shook his fist at them. Bugger off, he seemed to be saying. You're spooking the sheep.

Wyatt saw faces grin at him. Then the rotor tilted, the tail lifted, and the chopper left him in peace.

THIRTY-ONE

It was the longest afternoon of Raymond Trigg's life. Four hundred thousand bucks sitting there in the repair shop and it couldn't be touched until knock-off time.

He spent the hours until then answering his phone, paying bills and biting his nails. He thought the girls in reception looked at him oddly but he couldn't be sure. Happy was okay, Happy had valves to grind and punctures to mend. The problem—apart from the waiting—was Tobin. Tobin stuck out like a sore thumb in his shorts and singlet and orange shades. The girls knew who he was—the man who delivered or picked up parcels from time to time—but Trigg didn't want them asking why he was hanging around.

'I don't know why we don't just take the lot and disappear,' Tobin said. He'd been saying this since they got back. 'That's why I told you about the job in the first place.'

'You don't know the Mesics, my son. They'd track us down and we'd be found in little pieces. I'm not going to debate about it. Three hundred thousand will get the Mesics off our backs, and we split the rest. Except you still owe me twenty grand for the last few consignments.'

'Yeah, well, that pisses me off. It should be sale or return. I'm expected to fork out twenty thousand bucks for pills and videos, but no one's buying, the economy's too fucked.'

'Look, I'm busy, okay? Why don't you take in a movie?'

It took Tobin a moment to absorb this. 'A movie?'

'We got a twin cinema,' Trigg said. He was leafing through the *Mid-North Gazette*. 'Cinema One—"Three Men and a Baby".'

'Seen it. Heap of shit.'

'Cinema Two—"Twins".'

'Never heard of it.'

Trigg peered at the advertisement. 'Arnold Schwarzenegger's in it.'

Tobin scratched his jaw and screwed up his face. 'Might be all right.'

'Gets out at five,' Trigg said. 'Maybe if you had a beer or two after, by the time you get back here the girls would've gone home and we can start cracking the van.'

Tobin's face narrowed in suspicion. 'You wouldn't be pulling a swifty?'

'Don't be a moron. We can't do anything till knock-off time.'

Tobin flushed. 'Yeah, well,' he said, and he headed off down the street to the mall.

When he was gone, Trigg thought about the Steelgard van and the money. The doors wouldn't be a problem. The thermal lance and jaws-of-life gear would take care of the doors. After the money was removed, Happy would dismantle the CO cylinder, hose and tap he'd put in place when the van was last serviced.

Venables had been anxious about the gas. He'd wanted to know what sort it was. Trigg told him sleeping gas. Then he'd wanted to know how come it was necessary. We don't want the guard seeing any faces, hearing any voices, Trigg said. Venables frowned, hunting for holes in the story. When should I turn on the tap? he asked. As soon as you've left Vimy Ridge, Trigg told him.

Still Venables hadn't liked it. Was Trigg sure it would work? Was he sure the cops wouldn't think it was an inside job?

You trying to chicken out? Trigg had demanded. You want to go on paying me interest for the rest of your life? Do this little thing for me, old son, and all your debts are cancelled.

Stupid prick.

All that remained now was to clear up a few loose ends, get rid of the evidence, deliver the money to Melbourne.

Trigg was looking forward to that part of it. He'd rung to

say he was coming over. He had a plane ordered for seven that evening. Goyder Air Service didn't run to Lear Jets but they'd assured him they had a turbo-prop Beechcraft that was fast and comfortable. Get him to Melbourne before ten o'clock, they said. Well, the local graziers did this sort of thing all the time, flew interstate to the ram sales wearing their moleskins, Akubras and R. M. Williams elastic-sided boots, and Trigg didn't see why he shouldn't pose a bit too.

Except your average grazier these days doesn't carry three hundred grand around with him.

Trigg thought about how it would go at the other end. He could take a taxi to the Mesic compound, but something about that seemed low-class. He reached for the intercom.

'Liz?'

'Yes, Mr Trigg.'

'I want you to get on the blower and see if you can arrange a limo for me.'

'Pardon?'

'Doesn't have to be a stretch limo. An ordinary one will do, like a Jag. So long as it's black and there's a chauffeur and he's waiting when I touch down in Melbourne tonight.'

There was a long pause. Trigg waited. He knew the locals were a bit slow. It took them a while to take on board new notions like stretch limos, even though they saw them on TV all the time. 'Got that?' he asked.

'Yes, Mr Trigg.'

'Good girl.'

Drive up to the compound gates in the limo, wait while the guy at the gate calls ahead for permission to let him in, then creep slowly through the compound to the main house.

The compound. Trigg had never seen anything like it before. The Mesics had bought up an entire suburban block in Melbourne, knocked down most of the houses except one for the servants, erected two mansions—one for the old man, the other for Leo Mesic and his wife—planted a few trees, built a high fence around it, put in the latest alarm system and a few armed guards, and no one could touch them.

That was the way your top boys did it these days.

This time tomorrow, Trigg thought, the Mesics will be three hundred grand richer. They'll also be off my frigging back.

At five-thirty he left the office and went through to reception. Marg, as usual, had slipped away early. Liz was staring into space. 'How did you go?' he asked her.

'Sorry?'

It was always the same. He said it again, slowly, carefully. 'The limo. Were you able to line up a limo for me in Melbourne?'

Liz beamed. 'Sorry, yes, something called an SEL.'

Mercedes, Trigg thought. Nice.

'But I couldn't arrange one this end.'

Now it was Trigg's turn to look perplexed. 'Sorry?'

'I asked around. No one does chauffeur cars in Goyder.'

Trigg counted to ten. 'That's okay. I'll drive myself. You've done a good job.' He looked at his watch. 'Well, if you've finished for the day you might as well toddle off home.'

Liz got into a muddle over that but by five-forty he was alone. He went across to the service bay where Happy was greasing a Volvo. 'All set?'

Happy didn't reply. He usually didn't. He put down the wrench he was using, wiped his hands and together they crossed the lot to the panel-beating shed.

It was crowded in there. When the good folk of Goyder were asleep in their beds on Sunday evening, they intended to dump the truck with the van still aboard it into Hallam Gorge, but until then they had to edge around each other, avoiding the old-fashioned mechanics' pit in the floor. Next to the pit was a new hydraulic hoist, still in its packing case. Bags of cement were stacked against one wall.

Trigg and Happy dragged cutting equipment to the rear doors of the Steelgard van and started work. They had just cut out the lock on the Steelgard van when Tobin found them. He was beery and flatulent, wavering on his feet as he watched Happy prise open the doors. He burped. 'Wasn't your usual Arnie.'

This was too much for Trigg. He turned and snarled, 'What the hell are you on about?'

'The movie. Nothing like your usual Schwarzenegger.'

Trigg turned away from him in time to see the doors spring open. The guard lay sprawled on the floor of the van. There were steel cabinets built into the floor and walls. That's where the money would be.

Trigg thought he might as well do it now. In a single motion he picked up a steel mallet and swung around with it, adjusting for Tobin's height. The metal head was swinging upwards when it smacked under Tobin's jaw. Tobin dropped as if all the elasticity had gone out of him. Trigg hit him again to make sure, then tumbled him into the pit. He let Happy do the guard.

THIRTY-TWO

Wyatt spilled off the bike sometime in the middle of the afternoon. It was a bad fall, leaving him bruised and winded. Partly it was the change in the terrain. As he pushed farther south the grazing land gave way to cultivated land—wheat, oats, barley, peas, lucerne, all tightly sown in coarse, ploughed furrows. The Suzuki's front tyre hit irrigation piping concealed in thick lucerne. The handlebars were wrenched out of his grasp, and he was off. He landed heavily on his side, one leg twisted under the bike frame. He lay there for a minute, thinking how quiet it was without the engine screaming under him. The stubby lucerne, crushed and tangled under his cheek, smelt fresh and clean. He longed to stay there, but the exhaust pipe began to burn through his overalls.

He struggled free and stood up. It was more than the change in terrain, he realised. He'd been rough-riding the Suzuki for almost three hours and he was tired, his body so jarred that he didn't trust his judgement any more.

The spill helped him decide—he needed to rest, and he needed to find a car. He looked around. The farmland here was more closely settled. There was a town in the distance. A bitumen road went through it. Wyatt counted the traffic. There seemed to be a vehicle every minute or so.

There were other reasons why he should dump the bike. The cops would have found bike tracks at the farm by now. Sooner or later they'd compare notes with the chopper crew and realise that the figure they'd seen looking at his sheep hadn't been a farmer. They'd also got a good look at his face, so he'd have to do something about that soon as well. And he could smell petrol. Some had spilled onto the ground. He shook the bike:

there wasn't much in the tank. He would rather steal a car than a tankful of petrol for the bike.

He uprooted clumps of lucerne, covered the bike and set off across the paddocks on foot. He felt exposed. The sky above him was open, the flat land benign under the afternoon sun, but he knew it could turn bad quickly. Two men shot to death; signs of occupancy in an abandoned farmhouse nearby; a missing security van with up to half a million on board—it all added up to crusading cops, trigger-happy farmers and nervy civilians all over the state. The search would be big and thorough and there wouldn't be any second chances once they'd found him.

Wyatt also wanted to get his hands on a radio. The ABC and the commercial stations would be running hot with this story. He might learn things about the police operation that would help him escape the net, and he might hear if there had been any arrests—hear if Leah or Tobin had been nabbed, or anyone else from the other team. Information was like blood to Wyatt.

He was not sure of the next stage. He walked until he came to the town, stopping just short of it and skirting the edge until he came to a quarry carved like an ugly bite in a hill half a kilometre behind the town. From there he had a clear view of the main street and the grid of smaller streets on both sides of it. It looked to be bigger than Belcowie. It had two of everything. He thought if he waited long enough he'd see a lapse in someone's security.

The answer was a school bus. Soon after he settled down to wait, he heard three blasts of a siren. The sound carried clearly to him and he pinned down the school as the source. A few minutes later kids poured out of all the classrooms. Some boarded the three yellow buses parked with staff cars at the side of the administration block; the others walked or rode bicycles to houses in different parts of the town. As Wyatt watched, three men with briefcases left the administration block, boarded the buses and drove out of the town. Teachers, Wyatt thought, earning extra money driving a school bus.

He guessed that the buses did a run of the outlying farms and towns. Ninety minutes later, the first of the buses came back. This one parked outside the pub and Wyatt saw the driver go into the bar. The second bus parked outside a house on the other side of the town. But the third bus was delivered back to the schoolyard and the teacher driving it walked to his house from there.

Wyatt didn't wait. Within fifteen minutes he'd hot-wired the bus outside the school and was heading away from the town.

There were no roadblocks—he'd come too far south for that—but he was worried about his face. There would be an identikit of him by now. Cops would be at all the main stations, bus terminals and airports. He needed a bolthole, somewhere where he could rest and do something about his face. And get a radio.

But the country towns he was passing through were too small to provide that sort of cover. They'd be jumpy places too, he thought. So would the farms surrounding them. He needed to find a large place.

He entered Aberfeldie just as the street lights were coming on. The first indications were favourable, but he drove through slowly, to make sure. He was reminded of Goyder. Aberfeldie had the same range of motels, small businesses and flashing neon along the main street, the same sprawl of ugly new houses and flats at either end. There was even a mall. The town hall was as big as any he'd seen in Melbourne.

He had to get rid of the bus before he did anything. He didn't dump it in the street—it would be like a signpost to the police if he did that. He always left stolen vehicles where they couldn't be found until the trail was cold. Despite its size, the bus was easy to hide. He simply hid it in the open. He drove until he found the high school, then parked the bus outside the work-shop of a service station on the other side of the road. The mechanics would scratch their heads over it in the morning, and eventually someone would ring the school and ask what they wanted done with it, but by then he'd be long gone.

It was seven o'clock before Wyatt found somewhere to spend the night. He wasn't interested in a house—a house has neighbours who want to know what is going on. There are also neighbours in blocks of flats but they tend to come and go and expect others to come and go, so he wasn't expecting anyone to ask him his business there.

There were six units in the first block he examined. Most had their lights on and all had empty letterboxes. He moved on to the next block. Flats 2 and 6 had not claimed their letters yet. He rejected flat 2 when he heard someone answer the telephone. He climbed to flat 6, listened for half a minute, knocked on the door and listened again. Silence. He picked the lock and entered. There was no one home but the place felt lived in. Then he saw a movement in the corner. It was a cat, stretching awake in a basket on the floor.

Wyatt let himself out quickly and walked down the stairs and along to a single-storey block in the next street. These he rejected immediately. According to a sign by the driveway entrance, the flats were let to elderly parishioners of the Uniting Church. They would all be at home.

His luck improved at the third block of flats. The letterbox for flat 4 was crammed with junk mail. He climbed up to the second landing and tried the door. When no one answered his knock, he picked the lock and went in. This time there were no pets or signs that people had been there recently. The place felt as if it had been empty for several days. The rooms were tidy. The refrigerator had been switched off and the door left open. The garbage bin was empty and clean. He examined the bedroom and the bathroom. The clothing, jewellery and cosmetics indicated that a youngish man and woman lived there.

But how secure was he? He checked the calendar pinned to a cabinet door above the sink. Notes had been scribbled in the blank spaces under some of the dates. *Leave for Qld* had been written under a date at the beginning of the month and a bold blank line cancelled the next two weeks. At the end were the words *Arrive home*. Wyatt understood that he had the place for a week if he wanted it. He hoped the key hadn't been given to friends or relatives. He hoped the weather was fine in Queensland.

Before doing anything he turned on the transistor radio next to the toaster on the kitchen bench. According to the news, no arrests had been made yet. The money and the van were still missing. There was, however, evidence that several people had spent several days in an abandoned farmhouse not far from the area where the bodies were found. Police were broadening their search.

Wyatt switched off the radio and went into the bathroom. He stripped and washed at the sink, not in the shower, knowing how thin the walls were in these places, how noisy the plumbing. Then he went to work on his appearance. In the cabinet above the sink he found hair gel, an old razor, scissors, a comb and two boxes containing blonde hair-colouring cream and rubber gloves. He shaved first, removing not only the day's stubble but also his sideburns. Then he shortened his hair at the top, front and sides. Finally he applied the cream to his hair, leaving it on for almost an hour before rinsing it off. He looked curiously at himself in the mirror. He was fair-haired now, his features thin and drawn. He finished by wiping away water drops and stains with toilet paper and stuffing the paper into a plastic shopping bag.

In a bedroom drawer he found a tracksuit that was short in the leg but otherwise fitted him. Dresses, slacks, blouses and skirts took up most of the wardrobe space, but there were also some trousers and shirts and a couple of suits and sportscoats. The chest and waist sizes looked to be about right; he was too tired to check just now.

Finally he went into the kitchen to get something to eat. He didn't want to heat anything and release cooking smells, so he opened a tin of goulash and ate it cold from the tin. It had the consistency of glue. He washed and dried the spoon and put the empty tin in the plastic bag with the toilet paper.

Then he slept. He didn't need an alarm. His instincts would tell him when to wake.

He woke at dawn. He washed and shaved again, then combed gel through his hair and parted it in the middle. He dressed in a white shirt, plain tie and a dark grey suit. The trousers were short in the leg, but he reflected that that wasn't unusual in country towns. There were four pairs of shoes at the bottom of the wardrobe. All were too big for him. He put on two more pairs of socks and tried the grey suede shoes; they were soft and had a rubber sole and he figured that made more sense than stiff leather shoes. With the extra socks they fitted well.

He listened to the six o'clock news. The murders and the robbery were still the main items, but the situation was unchanged.

Then he wiped the flat for prints, cleared any mess he'd made, and bundled his dirty clothes into the shopping bag. The occupants of the flat would be puzzled by the missing clothes, but if nothing else was missing and the place untouched, they probably wouldn't report it. It wouldn't matter if they did; the trail would be cold by then.

Wyatt opened the door to the corridor and listened. No-one else seemed to be up. He let himself out quietly and walked down the street. The station was ten minutes walk away. He dumped the shopping bag in a rubbish bin along the way.

The air was cool. Not many cars were about. He got to the station a few minutes before seven o'clock. There were four cars in the car park. The platform was deserted and there were no cops in the waiting room or the ticket office. The only people he saw were the station master making coffee in a room next to the ticket office and a bleary-eyed man in the waiting room.

Wyatt looked at the timetable. There was an Adelaide train at 7.35 am. The return train got in at 6.30 that evening.

Twenty minutes later, there were eight more people waiting for the train. Most were women who appeared to be going to

Adelaide for a day's shopping, but there were also two men in suits. All were yawning. One of the men coughed repeatedly. Another smoked, ignoring the sign.

When the train came in they all stood up and walked onto the platform. Wyatt went into the men's. When the train was gone, he went out to the car park. There were now twelve cars parked along the fence. He chose a white Kingswood, knowing it was the easiest to break into and start. It wouldn't be missed until 6.30. By then he'd be holding a gun to Leah's head, asking what her story was.

THIRTY-THREE

He'd been in the implement shed. She had just shut the bike away, and was turning to cross the yard, when he'd pressed the gun into the base of her spine and said, 'Turn around slowly.'

She smelt cop. He wasn't dressed like one, and he wasn't acting like one, but she smelt cop all the same. It was the suspicion, worn like a layer of skin, the contempt, the swagger of the heavy limbs. He had clever eyes in the whitest skin she'd ever seen on anyone and the sort of cop expression she knew well—permanent bleakness and cynicism. The eyes seemed to sum her up and toss her out.

When he'd spoken again it was to ask where Wyatt was.

'Who?'

Dumb. He'd flashed the gun across her cheek, cutting the skin open. He didn't ask it again, just looked at her. 'You're expecting him,' he said flatly. 'We'll wait in the house. Move.'

She turned and they walked across the yard. She felt the gun brush her spine.

When they reached the house he prodded her. 'In the kitchen.'

So he knew the layout. She heard his footsteps on the verandah behind her and then he was crowding her as they went through the door.

At the centre of the room she turned to face him. 'Do you work for Jorge? Steelgard? Did you warn the van?'

His expression changed for the first time, showing puzzlement. 'What are you talking about?'

She stared at him. 'You hijacked our job, right?'

'I don't know what you're talking about. Is Wyatt coming or not?'

They had stared at each other then. She remembered noticing odd details, things that had nothing to do with who he was or what he was doing there. The shoes, first. They were brand new desert boots, looking soft and brushed, with pale crepe rubber soles. Then the clothes. He was wearing the sort of things a farmer would wear, except they lacked the patina of age and use. They looked creased and new. In fact, there was still a pin in the shirt collar.

He spoke again. 'Something went wrong?'

There didn't seem to be any harm in answering. 'The van didn't show.'

'Snyder, Wyatt, the other man—where are they?'

She stiffened at that. How did he know so much? She felt the bad feelings swamping her again: the job going wrong, Wyatt shooting Snyder, the sense that this was real and nothing else in her life, no matter how rotten, had been real.

'Tobin went home,' she said. 'Snyder's dead.'

He looked disgusted. 'How did that happen?'

'Wyatt shot him.'

The man nodded gloomily. Keeping the gun trained on her, he backed up to the window and looked out.

'I'll ask again—you're waiting for Wyatt?'

She risked a lie. 'No. The job went wrong and we split up and got out of there. Wyatt's gone.'

'Bullshit,' the man said flatly. He knocked her head back with the butt of his gun. Her jaws closed with a click, her front teeth nipping her tongue. She tasted blood. The pain made her head swim.

Then he pushed her to the floor and she sat with her back to the wall. She didn't look up at the man after that. There was a cruel irony in all this. The badness she'd felt washing around her after Wyatt shot Snyder had evaporated a minute after she'd ridden off on the bike. It didn't make the shooting any better but she'd begun to feel guilty about abandoning Wyatt. She'd turned the bike around and ridden to the farm to help him. She should have kept running.

At that moment the man said viciously, 'Jesus Christ. A helicopter.'

He was standing at the window. Leah stood up and joined him. At first she couldn't see anything, but then the helicopter changed direction and she recognised the familiar shape. It was a small helicopter, still some distance away. It changed direction again. She was puzzled about that until she realised it was sweeping the valley in a grid pattern.

'We're getting out,' the man said.

'How?'

He jerked his head toward the back of the house. 'I've got a car.'

'You don't need me.'

The man looked her full in the face and grinned. 'Sweetheart,' he said, 'you're taking me home to wait for Wyatt.'

THIRTY-FOUR

Letterman directed her into arid country north-east of Burra. The map was spread over his lap, concealing the pistol trained at her thigh. Now and then he moved, dial-hunting on the car radio. He spoke only once in the first hour, asking her where she lived. She told him. There was no point in trying to deceive him. With all the police activity around, they both needed a bolthole.

A regional station picked up the hijack and killings story first. By four o'clock the ABC and all the Adelaide commercial stations had it. Police were sealing the area. They expected an early arrest. But Leah knew it was a big area to seal and Letterman—he'd finally told her his name—was steering them through a land of sand-drifts and mirages. It was clear to her that they were outside the search area. Here and there she saw roadside gates and a distant tin roof on a saltbush plain. When finally they came to a junction of dusty baked roads in a clearing in the mallee scrub, she knew what he had in mind. Morgan, the sign said. The River Murray. Letterman was intending to follow the river to Murray Bridge, then branch off for the Adelaide Hills.

Four o'clock. Five. Six. More information kept filtering through about the dead men and the missing van, but no names had been released and no arrests reported.

Letterman spoke. He looked up at her and said, 'What do you think?'

She knew what he meant. 'He got away.'

Letterman nodded. 'Yes.'

'What makes you think he'll come to my place?'

'Nothing makes me think it. It's the only option I've got.'

She waited. When he didn't follow this up she asked, 'And if the cops gaol him first?'

The reply was flat and certain. 'I can still get him there.'

'What do you want with him? We didn't get any money. Is it personal?'

'No.'

'What, then?'

Letterman shrugged. 'It's a job. He trod on some toes.'

They lapsed into silence again. Eventually they reached the river and turned south. The sun was low in the sky. Leah turned on. the headlights.

'What are they paying you?'

'Fifty thousand.'

'I can pay you that. I'll pay you more if you like. Just drop the matter and leave us alone.'

'I can't do that,' Letterman said.

She glanced at him. Letterman was staring ahead. The pistol hadn't moved. She couldn't see it under the map but she sensed its probing snout. She looked at the road again.

'Watch your driving,' Letterman said.

She wanted him to say what he intended to do if Wyatt didn't show up. She knew the answer—he'd kill her whether Wyatt showed up or not—but she wanted to hear him say it.

'What if he slips interstate? What if he's injured somewhere? What if the cops have him but they're not saying?'

'You talk too much.'

He was curiously asexual. It was more than the white skin— he lacked any sort of sensual dimension. Trying to distract him in that way would be a waste of time.

It was late when they reached her house. Most of the neighbouring houses were in darkness. Leah felt a surge of hope. Wyatt could be in there, waiting for them. She surreptitiously slid her hand to the horn button.

Letterman hit her, slamming the pistol barrel across her wrist. The pain made her stomach churn. Her fingers seemed to clench lifelessly as if she didn't own them.

Letterman opened his door and stepped out, pulling her

across the seat towards him. When they were outside the car he pushed her onto the ground next to the front bumper and cuffed her wrist to it. 'Not a sound,' he said.

She watched him enter her yard and walk around the side of the house. She shivered, fear and the chilly night air clamping themselves to her skin and bones. Far away on the freeway, a truck snarled through the gears. A garden tap dripped nearby.

When Letterman came back it was through the front door. He hadn't asked her for her keys, so he must have got in by forcing a window or the back door lock. She hadn't heard anything. If Wyatt had been inside he wouldn't have heard anything either. She asked, her voice low: 'Was he in there?'

Letterman knelt to uncuff her. 'No.'

He took her into the house and cuffed her wrist to her ankle while he built a large fire in the grate and lit it. Then he took her into the kitchen and cuffed her to the refrigerator door. He didn't speak, didn't explain himself. He found the frozen fish fillets in the freezer and the vegetables in the bottom compartment and cooked them separately in the microwave. He sneered at her rack of Queen Adelaide riesling but opened one and poured two glasses. Then he took her into the lounge again and they ate in front of the fire, the plates balanced on their knees. At eleven o'clock he took her upstairs, cuffed her to her bed, unplugged her bedside telephone and turned out her light.

She didn't see him again until the next morning. He uncuffed her and waited while she showered and changed her clothes. He looked fresh and rested. He'd slept behind the couch in the corner of the ground floor lounge room. She saw blankets and a pillow there when they went through to the kitchen.

'He's not coming,' she said.

'Shut up.'

Letterman didn't speak to her all day, just listened to the hourly news broadcasts on the radio and cleaned his gun. At midday he went out and came back with copies of the *Advertiser* and the *News*. Both carried front page stories of the killings and the van that had vanished. He passed her the *Advertiser* when he'd finished with it. There were photographs of the farm and the Holden utility with its doors open. A detailed map showed the area of the police net. But according to the radio a stolen school bus had been found abandoned in Aberfeldie, and police were now concentrating their attention further afield.

'He's coming,' Letterman said.

'He won't come here.'

'He's coming.'

The air was cold in the house. After lunch Letterman lit another fire and they sat in front of it through the afternoon and into the evening. If it hadn't been for the handcuffs and Letterman getting up to peer out of the window every fifteen minutes, they might have been waiting in a counterfeit of married-couple ease or indifference. Leah almost forgot who Letterman was and why he was there. The plantation trees set up a moaning as the wind rose. Smoke from the chimney blew back into the room. They both coughed occasionally and around them the old house seemed to stretch and creak as if it were breathing.

They went to the kitchen, cooked dinner, took it back to the lounge room again. A storm seemed to be blowing up outside. Smoke made their eyes water. Racking coughs shook Letterman every few minutes. It was the only indication of vulnerability that Leah had seen him display. Yet she wasn't fooled by it. She felt a heightened sense of the coldness and patience inside him. She saw his face form and re-form in the firelight.

But something was wrong with the fire. Letterman rubbed his eyes. He coughed. Her own eyes were streaming. The air was heavy with smoke. Letterman looked past her at the fire, frowned, coughed again. He got up and prodded the logs with a poker. Smoke was rolling out now, choking coils of it, dimming the light and starving them of oxygen.

Letterman got up and uncuffed her. 'He's here.'

Then the lights went out.

THIRTY-FIVE

There were lights on inside but the curtains were closed and the windows and doors were locked, so Wyatt had no clear sense of what he might find until he heard the cough. It was a man's cough.

He'd already examined the car. He couldn't judge colours properly under the streetlight but the dust coating the Valiant seemed familiar enough. He'd been sneezing it for the past month. He knelt, keeping the car between himself and the house. There were clumps of grass caught in the dust flaps and bumper bars.

He wondered who the man was. He didn't think it would be Tobin. Leah had better taste than that. He guessed it would be somebody from the other team. Not that he cared either way now. He'd found them. He'd kill them, get his money, start somewhere new. It wasn't something Wyatt intended to waste time thinking about. He'd been crossed, that was all he needed to know.

He was pleased about the stormy wind. It masked the creak of the gate, his footsteps, his examination of the doors and windows.

He was at the side of the house when a downdraft of wind caught him. It was laden with smoke, burning the back of his throat. He looked up at the chimney. He thought about the cough.

The roofline was flat and low above the porch at the rear of the house. By climbing the paling fence at the side he was able to leap onto it. He landed lightly but the old struts underneath the roofing iron moaned under his weight. He made for the upper roof area, into which the upstairs rooms had been built, climbed onto it, crawled to the peak and clutched the chimney.

Wyatt hadn't been sure how he would block the chimney—throw his suit coat over it perhaps—but when he stood up next to it he discovered a lightweight metal plate hanging from a short chain. It was a cap to keep the birds out in the summer months. He placed it over the hole and dropped it into place. Someone in the next house opened a back door, called 'Puss, puss, puss,' and went inside again.

Wyatt climbed down the way he'd come. The fuse box was on the front verandah. He opened it, switched off the power and tossed the fuses away.

Inside the house they were coughing. Someone bumped into a piece of furniture and he heard glass shatter. The reading light, he thought.

Tying a handkerchief about his nose and mouth, he opened the front door with his key and slipped into the house. He could smell the smoke, although little had leaked into the rest of the house as yet. He paused at the lounge room doorway, his back to the wall, his .38 extended ready to fire.

He guessed they'd be too smart to pose themselves in front of the fire. He also knew he'd be illuminated by firelight if he tried to come through the door in the ordinary manner. The moment he appeared he'd be shot. His only chance was to come in fast and throw himself down to one side. If someone fired a shot the muzzle flash would give away their position. He could wait them out but one of them might escape through a window and come in behind him.

Wyatt tensed himself and charged through the door. He dived to his right, rolled, and stood half-crouching.

He heard a snuffle as someone fired at him. The slug smacked into the wall above his head.

Found you, he thought, focusing on the muzzle flash. Two shapes, Leah and a bulkier figure with a gun. Wyatt swung his .38 around, aimed, tightened his finger on the trigger.

And stepped on something and lost his footing. He landed

on his back, knocking the breath from his body. His .38 skidded under a chair. The fireplace poker grumbled away from him across the wooden floor. The two figures disappeared through the open door.

The seconds passed. Wyatt got up from the floor, holding to the back of a chair until he could breathe normally again. The fall, coming so soon after his fall from the bike, made him feel slowed down and clumsy.

He was at least a minute behind them.

He closed the door, sealing in the smoke, and stood in the hall, listening and thinking. Without the light from the fire the house was in absolute darkness. Every curtain was drawn. Would the gunman open them to give himself light to shoot by? Wyatt doubted it. He'd feel too vulnerable.

People in darkness are very sensitive to another person's presence. Wyatt was relying on that as well as his hearing. He crept down the hallway and stood for some time at the open door to the study. He breathed slowly, quietly, extending his inhalations and exhalations so that the tiny sounds he made did not sound like breathing. He listened for exertions and tension in the other two.

He went through all the downstairs rooms doing this. They were empty. He looked at the stairs. Ten minutes had gone by but when Wyatt climbed the stairs he stopped for long periods on each step. He wanted to be certain. He was also trying to read the gunman. Was he capable of waiting immobile for hours at a time? Or would he want to precipitate action, come out shooting? Wyatt reached the top step. He stood there listening, breathing shallowly, for five minutes.

They were betrayed by a watch. Wyatt heard the faint double beep that indicated the passing of another hour. What hour? Ten, Wyatt guessed. He advanced cautiously to the doorway of the main bedroom.

The angle was bad. He had to get to the other side of the door. But he wondered if the gunman had adjusted to the dark by now, letting him register any shape crossing the gap. Wyatt's best chance was to present a confusing shape. He dived, rolled and got to his feet again. There was a shot as he passed by the door, but it went high.

Suddenly there were five more shots. Wyatt heard the slugs punch through the plasterboard wall, spaced at groin height. The last one emerged a hand's breadth from his hip. He didn't move.

Leah yelled out: 'Quick, his gun's empty.'

It was a ruse. But the fact that they were trying it could mean they were off-balance for a moment. Wyatt threw himself through the door and came up with his .38 aimed and ready.

Leah moaned. 'He's got a knife.'

Wyatt focused on her, a dim shape against the curtain. The man stood behind her, one arm around her torso, the other at her neck. In struggling they had disturbed the curtain a little. Weak moonlight lit the room; Wyatt could see it glinting on the blade under Leah's jaw.

'Throw your gun down,' the man said, 'or I cut her throat.'

'Go ahead,' Wyatt said, 'cut.'

He could hear the next-door neighbours beneath the window outside. 'Should we knock and see?' one of them said. 'It's just the wind,' the other said. Wyatt looked around the room, sizing up the walls and furniture abstractedly. The gunman had only his arms and half his face showing. A voice outside said, 'Come inside for God's sake.' A door banged.

'Drop it,' the man said again, 'or she dies.'

'Fine,' Wyatt said.

It didn't matter to Wyatt which one he killed first. Killing Leah first would give him a clear shot at the man. But the man had the weapon. He might throw the knife. Wyatt raised the .38. He turned a little to one side, held his arm fully out, and pulled the trigger. It was quick, practised, tight, like a dance step.

The bullet caught the man in the throat, jerking him back against the wall. The arm around Leah stiffened, then relaxed, and she pushed free of him. The blood welled in his throat.

Wyatt said nothing. He turned the gun on Leah.

But she was a bad target. The gunman, sitting on the floor now, raised the knife to throw it. As Wyatt followed Leah with the gun, he saw her dart down, wrestle the knife away, and jerk back.

That was when he saw the handcuff. He took his finger from the trigger but kept the .38 trained on her. The man on the floor coughed, a liquid sound in his throat, and fell sideways, twitching once or twice.

Leah looked at Wyatt. 'You might have hit me.'

Wyatt nodded. 'But I didn't.'

She held her arms around herself. 'But you might have.'

Wyatt knew that he was being unfair. He knew how his coldness discouraged people and coloured the way he saw the world. He pocketed the gun as a way of saying that he was disarming himself, then slumped back against the wall to wait, knowing it was too soon to touch her.

Leah shivered, her arms wrapped around her chest. The handcuffs swung on her left wrist. 'I'll be all right in a minute.'

'I doubted you,' Wyatt said. 'I shouldn't have.'

She didn't approach him but let go of her arms and seemed to notice him properly. 'You've changed your appearance,' she said. She shivered. 'Everything's weird.'

Wyatt sat on the bed and pointed at the body. 'Did he tell you anything?'

'He said his name was Letterman and he was hired to kill you. Apparently you trod on somebody's toes.'

Wyatt gestured in frustration. 'A Sydney mob. It's so stupid. Clearly they're not going to let go of it, so now I'll have to talk to them.'

Leah sat next to him on the bed. 'Talk to them? Will they listen?'

'They'll listen.'

'Do you know who?'

'I'll find out.'

They were silent, looking at the body. 'He was waiting at the farm,' Leah said. 'Snyder had been in contact with him.'

'That figures. It's my guess Letterman put the word out offering big bucks to anyone who knew where to find me.'

'He must have followed Snyder from Melbourne.'

Wyatt nodded. 'And he wouldn't have paid Snyder the full

amount until he was sure he'd found me. That's why Snyder was so keen for us to go back to the farm instead of running. He'd missed out on the payroll—he didn't want to miss out completely.'

By now their shoulders were touching. It calmed Wyatt and seemed to calm Leah. She rested more heavily against him. 'What went wrong?' she asked. 'Judging by the way Snyder and Letterman acted, they were just as surprised as we were.'

Wyatt told her what he'd found on the road. 'They hijacked our job, copying it detail for detail.'

Leah looked closely at his face. 'Because I brought in Tobin,' she said, 'you thought I was behind the whole thing?'

'It's happened before. Tell me about him.'

She rolled her shoulders in embarrassment. 'You know that guy you got the bike from, the one who pissed you off? I got Tobin's name from him. I thought you'd get mad if you knew I'd gone to him again.'

Wyatt didn't push it. Tobin was a distributor of bootleg booze, videos and cigarettes. Maybe his supplier was behind it. He put his arm around Leah's shoulders. She made a noise in her throat.

Then he felt her stiffen and jerk away from him. 'I can't stay in the room with him there.'

She got to her feet and went downstairs. Wyatt changed into his own clothes and shoes, the searched Letterman's pockets until he'd found the keys to the handcuffs. But something about the big man's shape bothered him. A minute later he was counting out thirty thousand dollars from Letterman's moneybelt. He pocketed twenty thousand and went downstairs. The bottom half of the house was full of smoke. He gave Leah the keys and ten thousand dollars. 'Take the cuffs off,' he said. 'Pour yourself a drink. I'll be back in a moment.'

Checking that no one was standing in the garden next-door, he climbed to the roof and removed the chimney cap. When he got back inside Leah had opened all the doors and windows.

She handed him a glass of Scotch. It was fiery and reviving. 'What do we do now?' she asked.

'Dump the body,' Wyatt said simply, 'and get our money back.'

She drank deeply from the glass. 'Just like that.'

'Did the neighbours see Letterman?'

'No.'

'All the same, you'd better have a story ready in case they ask about him or his car or the noise tonight. Meanwhile help me put him in the boot. I'll dump him and the car in the city somewhere.'

Leah had the look of someone who knows that the relaxing is still a long way off. 'What if they ask me about you? What if they recognise your picture?'

'I look different now and I kept out of sight whenever I stayed here. But the short answer is, distract them. Don't just say I'm a brother or something, you have to make them feel embarrassed for asking. Tell them I'm your Jesuit priest brother, your detective cousin.' He put down his glass. 'I'd better be going. Help me with Letterman.'

They loaded the body into the boot of the Valiant. The wind-tossed street was dark; no one saw them.

'Let me go with you,' Leah said.

The coldness grew in Wyatt again. 'No. Wait here.'

'You think I'll get in the way,' she said. 'You think I'll get hurt.'

He was uncomprehending. He hadn't been considering her at all. He knew only that he'd been crossed and he had to do something about it and he could best do it alone. 'Get some rest,' he said. 'Air the house. Reassure the neighbours.'

He got into the driver's seat of Letterman's car and wound down the window. Leah put her face to the gap and clasped the top of the glass. 'Are you going to Tobin's?'

He started the engine. 'It's the only link we have.' He looked at her strained face. He was unused to smiling. He touched her wrist briefly. 'Okay?'

She stood back. 'Good luck.'

Luck wouldn't come into it but he said thanks and started the engine.

He drove out of the hills and down into the centre of Adelaide. It was midnight when he passed through Enfield and the streets were quiet. The industrial estate was deserted. Cheerless lights were burning outside most of the buildings, throwing shadows into the door and window recesses. He turned off the headlights and drove once around the perimeter. There was no sign of security guards but he knew a patrol would be along later. He remembered seeing the Mayne Nickless calling cards in Tobin's doorframe.

Wyatt parked the Valiant behind a stack of empty crates. Tobin's office and shed were in darkness but he approached quietly, keeping to the shadows. He got to the side wall and waited, listening for two minutes. The side window was locked. He checked the front door. It was also locked. A thumb tacked note said, 'Back next week.' Scribbled under it were the words, 'No cash on premises.'

There were no external indications that Tobin had fitted an alarm system. Wyatt cast back in his mind to the day when he and Leah had first met him. He was sure there were no wires, cameras or electric eyes.

The glass in the side window was fused to wire netting, and he didn't want to be spotted at the front of the building, so he broke in through the back door.

Tobin wasn't there. The air was stale, as if no one had been in the place for several days.

Wyatt began a search of the office. There was nothing else he could do. Checking that no headlights had appeared outside, he turned on Tobin's planet lamp and adjusted the shade until it was an inch from the desktop. In the muted light he began to go through the drawers and files.

He didn't know what he was looking for but he knew he'd found it when he opened the grubby ruled desk diary and learned what kind of company Tobin had been keeping.

THIRTY-SEVEN

The car was legitimate so there was no point in stealing one. His face and clothing were different so he wasn't expecting second looks from nosy cops and civilians. But he'd be put away for life if he was found with a body in the boot. Checking again for Mayne Nickless patrols, Wyatt dragged Letterman inside and dumped him in a back room.

It turned midnight as he drove away from the industrial estate. He went left at Gepps Cross and settled in for the two-hour haul to Goyder. The traffic was light—a lonely taxi, a couple of panel vans drag-racing away from the lights, a big semitrailer with Western Australian plates. If Wyatt were an ordinary citizen he might have been tempted to put his foot down. He didn't. He slowed for yellow lights, used his indicators, sat just under the posted speed limits. He turned on the heater and set the radio to an all-night jazz program. Thirty minutes after dumping Letterman he had left the city lights behind and was driving through orchard country lit by the stars in the black sky.

Trigg must have thought all his Christmases had come at once when Tobin came to pick up his regular consignment of bootleg videos, booze and cigarettes and told him about the Steelgard hit. Trigg was already linked to Steelgard: Wyatt remembered seeing the Steelgard vans refuelling in Goyder, remembered the day he saw Venables talking to Trigg in Belcowie.

He pushed on through the dark farmland, fitting the pieces together. Now and then he passed through small towns. At night they appeared to flatten their bellies to the ground. The shopfronts seemed to hide under drooping verandahs. Dewy cars turned their backs away and the street lamps were meek and blanketed. It was all depressing. Wyatt preferred the open road, where he had the sensation of riding across the roof of the world.

He reached Goyder at two o'clock in the morning. Trigg Motors was lit up like a strip of pinball parlours. The big Ford sign glowed blue and white like a sail above the entrance and someone had been liberal with fluorescent paint on the showroom windows. The cars bared their chrome teeth at Wyatt as he cruised slowly along the front of the building. He turned right, and right twice again, circling the block. There was no sign of life—no security guards, cranky Alsatians or randy teenagers.

A couple of cars were parked outside the service bay. Wyatt guessed they'd been left there for a service or a tune-up in the morning. He parked Letterman's Valiant next to them and got out, quietly closing the driver's door behind him.

He ignored the administration block. The money might be stashed away there but first he wanted to satisfy himself that he was right about what had happened a day and a half ago.

He started with the buildings at the rear of the block—two corrugated-iron sheds, each large enough to hold a truck, and a small prefab hut next to an iron shipping container. The prefab building was raised a foot off the ground. It had aluminium frame doors and windows and two cement steps leading to the front door. The windows were curtained in some frilly domestic material. It puzzled Wyatt until he heard the unmistakable squeak of bedsprings. Someone was asleep in there.

It wasn't the sort of place Trigg would live in. A guard, mechanic or odd-job man, Wyatt thought.

It told him to go slow and quiet. He crossed to the first of the long sheds. There were several windows high off the ground, and a roller door and a small metal door, both padlocked.

He tried the second shed. It was the same as the first. He knew both sheds would have a legitimate purpose—major mechanical repairs, panel-beating, spray-painting—but there were no signs up.

He circled the second shed, looking at the ground. He

rejected the first piece of wire as being too thick. The second seemed about right. He was fashioning it into a hooked shape when the sky seemed to fall on him. Strong hands grabbed him by the collar and belt and ran him head-on into the wall of the shed. He collapsed onto his knees and toppled over. Someone searched his pockets and found the .38. A boot thudded hard into his stomach and stamped on his fingers.

Wyatt looked up, feeling pain tug inside him. Blood ran from his scalp into his eyes. He coughed and focused on the figure who had hit him.

The man had no neck. His head was like a knob squeezed from a piece of rock. He was tall and watched Wyatt in a loose-muscled way. Despite his size he looked fast and flexible. He wore overalls and had the unhappiest expression Wyatt had ever seen on anybody.

Wyatt wondered about his .38. He guessed the big man had it tucked away in his overalls. He started to get to his feet, wondering if he'd be allowed to get that far. When nothing happened he realised the big man wanted a bit of sport with him.

The big man had the advantage of size. Wyatt hoped to make it a disadvantage by getting him tired. He edged away from the wall and began to circle around, goading him into wasted effort.

The big man was having none of it. He simply stayed on the spot, turning with small movements as Wyatt wasted energy on the outer circle.

Wyatt went on the offensive. He darted in, feinted with his left hand and sidearmed with his right. Instead of crushing the big man's windpipe the flat of his hand glanced off the thick upper arm. He felt a jabbing blow to the cut on his head.

Wyatt retreated, knowing the big man would work on that cut if he could. He circled again, skipping from one foot to the other like a boxer, holding himself tight, looking for an opening. He darted in, squared up as if to repeat his earlier mistake, then dropped to his knees and punched his left fist hard under the big man's belt.

Again he stepped back and circled. He saw that he'd hurt the big man. There was a rictus grin of pain. The breathing sounded forced. Wyatt danced in, landed hard blows to the big man's eyes, backed off. He did it again. The big man shook his head, baffled, but never took his eyes off Wyatt. Wyatt watched the massive arms, waiting for them to drop, a sign of fatigue. Wyatt felt good now, concentrated, his breathing and movements rhythmic and loose.

He went in a third time, going for the eyes again. The big man managed a stinging blow to Wyatt's ribs, but Wyatt knew his own punches were beginning to do real damage. This time he stepped just out of range, then in again before the man realised he wasn't circling out of reach again. The man blocked with his forearms but Wyatt was expecting that. He turned side on and lashed the side of his shoe down the big man's shin bones. It was hard and sharp and caught him by surprise. Wyatt saw him curl and tighten as if he'd bitten into a lemon.

He took advantage of that and went hard at the man's head, a succession of rapid punches left and right. His aim was to confuse—make the man dizzy, blur his vision, make his head ring. It was working. Wyatt stepped back out of reach. The big man was soaked with sweat, swaying, shaking his head as if something were clinging to it. Blood had run into his eyes. Ribbons of mucus clung to his lips and chin.

Wyatt was going to finish him off and search for a key when the voice came out of the darkness behind him. It called him old son and told him that was enough. What convinced Wyatt was the rifle barrel behind his ear.

THIRTY-EIGHT

'Hap?' Trigg said. 'You okay?'

The man known as Happy spat blood on the ground and wiped his sleeve across his eyes. He seemed to clear his mind quickly. He reached into a pocket of his overalls and pulled out Wyatt's .38. Wyatt watched him, expecting a pay-back, but Happy simply stood there as if waiting for orders. When Trigg said, 'Unlock the shed,' Happy did it as if none of his motivations were his own. He came back and stood next to Trigg and when Trigg told him to take Wyatt into the shed and tie him up, the big hands were firm and efficient, no more than that.

They used nylon rope and propped Wyatt on a scarred wooden chair next to a steel-topped bench that ran against the wall at the back of the shed. Most of the space was taken up by the bogus Brava truck with the Steelgard van still on its tray. The cement floor was spotted with oil and grease. Crash-repair tools were stacked against the walls and a new hydraulic hoist had been bolted to a fresh slab of cement. Pictures of bodybuilders had been clipped from magazines and taped to a chipboard panel above the bench. An outdated Michelin calendar curled from a nail at one end of it.

Trigg propped the rifle against the bench. He put his hands on his hips and looked at Wyatt. The little man resembled a furious sparrow. His hair seemed to puff with frustration. 'Who the fuck are you? No, let me guess—fucking Wyatt.'

Wyatt hadn't intended to speak. He wanted to provoke Trigg. But he also wanted information. 'Where's Tobin?'

This seemed to encourage Trigg's frustration. He pointed irritably at the hydraulic hoist bolted to the cement slab. 'Under there with the guard. If I'd've known you were going to show up I'd've waited before we filled it in.' He shook his head. 'Jesus Christ. Where the fuck am I going to stash you, eh? Answer me that.'

Wyatt studied him bleakly. Thugs like Trigg made it hard for the professionals. They were vicious and stupid and left a trail of unnecessary bodies behind. He counted: Venables, Tobin, the guard—and soon he'd be the fourth.

He looked at the floor where the pit had been. If the bodies were never found he knew what the police line would be: the guard did it and disappeared with the money. He turned back to Trigg. 'You hijacked my job. That money's mine.'

Coming from anyone else they would have sounded like playground words. But Wyatt always meant what he said. He also operated under the belief that stealing another man's job was dangerous. It led to unnecessary resentment and speculation. It meant you couldn't trust anyone the next time you wanted help, advice or equipment. He wasn't expecting Trigg to give him back the money—he was simply stating a fact.

Trigg seemed to be distracted by the claim. He said, frowning, 'I owed some money to the mob,' and took Happy by the arm. 'You can have him to play with in a minute, my son, after we check around outside.'

They went out. They would be back when they found the car and nothing else to worry about. That's when the beating would start.

Wyatt stood and hopped two steps to the bench. He rejected the oily invoices and the horse-racing liftout from the Adelaide *News*. The box of matches would be better for what he had in mind. For a moment he considered burning the rope, but rejected it as painful and time-consuming. Instead he turned his back, lifted his hands and grabbed the matchbox. By bending over slightly he was able to keep his hands raised while he tipped the matches on to the floor and tore the matchbox into small strips. Then he turned around again, kicked the matches under the bench and bent his mouth to the bench top. With his tongue he drew the strips of cardboard into his mouth. He chewed them a little until they were moist and malleable, then manoeuvred separate pieces under his top and bottom lips and inside each cheek. He knew that Happy would go for the head first. The cardboard wads would save his teeth for a while, minimise the damage to the inside of his mouth.

Wyatt hopped back to the chair and sat down in it. Trigg and the big man came back a few minutes later. Trigg started with questions. 'Where are the others? How much do they know?'

Wyatt stared at him dully.

'Okay, Hap,' Trigg said.

Wyatt looked up. There was no moral light in the big man's gloomy eyes. Happy stepped forward and smashed his fist into Wyatt's face. He did it again. The battering was skilful and hard. To help withstand the pain Wyatt made himself neutral, separate from the fists and the damage. He made eye contact with Trigg and didn't let go of it. He said nothing and tried to avoid involuntary sounds. He let his body go loose and yielding, knowing the pain would be worse if he were stiff and tense. Unnoticed by Happy he was breathing deeply and evenly. This helped him turn inwards, turn off from the fists and pain. He was also helped by what was happening to Happy. The big man no longer seemed uninvolved. The pressure and rhythm of his blows grew uneven, telling Wyatt that he was beginning to unhinge. It was becoming a personal thing to Happy. If he'd been punching regularly and systematically, Wyatt would have found the punishment more damaging.

The beating went on even after he toppled onto the floor. After a while Happy stood back, breathing heavily. Wyatt felt himself slipping in and out of consciousness. He coughed bloodied cardboard out of his mouth and heard the roar of the sea in his head. He could feel grit and grease where his cheek touched the floor. He knew that Trigg was saying something, but the voice was far away.

When he woke up he knew he'd been out for a few hours.

They'd taken the ropes off and he was lying on a foam rubber mattress. The air was stuffy. He tried to sit up but the pain tore through him and he blacked out. When he woke again the pain was still there, like a bird diving its beak into his body. In films the hero always gets up. Wyatt knew about real pain, how it stays with you. Taking it very slowly, he sat up.

The absolute lack of light puzzled him until he realised he'd been locked in the shipping container. He reached out a hand and touched the nearest wall. It had been insulated on the in-side—from the heat, he supposed, but he also knew it meant he could make all the noise he wanted and no one would hear him. He didn't risk standing yet. He slid along the perimeter of the container. At the back he found a stack of plastic boxes the size of Gideon Bibles. Videos. There was also a refrigerator with a lock on it.

Some time later they came to check on him. Blinding sun-light came through the door and Happy was there, holding a torch, the .38 and a glass of water. He turned on the torch and closed the door behind him. 'Drink,' he said, placing the glass on the floor.

Wyatt took small sips of the water. His mouth was dry and he had a raging thirst but he knew he'd vomit if he gulped the water. Happy, he noticed, was staring at him curiously, as if last night's fight and beating had bonded them in some way.

Wyatt tried to speak, coughed, tried again. 'Is it Saturday?'

Happy nodded.

'Why don't you just kill me?'

Happy considered the question carefully. 'Too many people. Sunday.'

Wyatt deciphered this. They were waiting for when it was quiet, no customers, no one shopping in the main street. It could also mean they intended to move him. 'Happy?' Wyatt said. 'Where's the money?'

The voice rumbled like sludge sliding off a shovel. 'I've got my share.'

'I know. Where did the boss take the rest of it?'

'Mesic,' the big man said.

Wyatt knew that name. It was a name in the Melbourne papers and it meant rackets and killings. The cops had given up on the street crimes to concentrate on tax evasion. They weren't getting far there, either. Not that Wyatt cared about any of that. Now that he knew who to go after and what to expect, he was starting to work out how to get his money back.

It didn't strike him as unrealistic to be thinking like this. The Mesics had his money and he wanted it back, that's all he cared about. It didn't occur to him to think that he wouldn't succeed, that he wouldn't be alive to do it.

'Hap?' he said. 'Trigg got a lot of money from that van, but you did most of the dirty work. I bet he paid you peanuts.'

'I know what you're trying to do,' Happy said. 'It won't work.'

It was the longest speech Wyatt had heard the big man make. He closed his eyes, shutting him out. A few minutes later Trigg came in. Wyatt looked up. Muscles were working around Trigg's mouth and eyes. His colour was high. 'Bloody tyre-kickers, that's all I get these days. Come on, Hap, we've got work to do.' He grinned at Wyatt. 'Plenty of fuck-tapes here, my son, a fridge full of pills. Pity they're no good to you.'

'Stay away from holes in the ground, Hap,' Wyatt said. 'Don't turn your back on the little turd.'

'Shut up, moron,' Trigg said.

When they were gone Wyatt checked the door. As he expected, it was a waste of time. He lay back and wondered if psychology would get him out of this.

THIRTY-NINE

He lay there for thirty-six hours. Happy checked on him from time to time, giving him water and food. They had their short-hand conversations but Happy wouldn't be drawn. Wyatt gave up trying to turn the big man against Trigg and lay in the darkness, adjusting to the silence.

His sleep was fitful. He felt cold during the night and the thin mattress was uncomfortable. On Sunday morning when Happy came to check on him he complained about it. 'Some cushions or a chair, Hap.'

What Happy did with his face was close to a grin. 'Not worth it,' he said.

Wyatt shrugged. 'Tell me, Hap—how will you do it? Dig another pit?'

Happy shook his massive head. 'Accident. Hallam Gorge.'

Hallam Gorge was an ugly buckling of the earth's plates a few kilometres north of Goyder. Wyatt had driven around it one day when he was working with Brava Construction's surveyor. At one point the road narrowed and all that lay between it and a sheer drop of half a kilometre was a white guard rail. He knew what Trigg and Happy had in mind now and he could see the appeal of it. There would be no one around when they left later that night. On Monday morning someone would see the hole in the guard rail and call the cops. The cops would find the wreckage of the truck and the van at the bottom, Wyatt's body at the wheel. They'd be able to close this part of the investigation. They'd assume Wyatt had been holed up in the area and was pulling out again when he misjudged a curve and ran off the road. They'd assume that left only the guard, and he would have the money. They'd go through the usual channels, checking flight lists, putting the guard's photo on the wire. They'd trace Wyatt back to Brava—that's if he had any skin left on his face after plunging half a kilometre down a cliff face.

'Where's Trigg?' he asked.

'Home.'

'Nice place? Does all right for himself does he, while you live in a shithole?'

Happy's features grew a few degrees warmer. 'I got simple tastes,' he said as he went out.

Trigg turned up late on Sunday afternoon, checked on Wyatt, left him in darkness again. Wyatt could sense the decent people of the little city settling into sleep in front of their TV screens. Work tomorrow. Early to bed.

At 2 a.m., when the night was at its blackest, Trigg and Happy came to get him. Trigg held the .38 on him while Happy clasped his arms. Parked outside the doors of the shipping container was a roomy, late model family sedan with a sloping rear window. The boot was open.

'Get in,' Trigg said.

'I get claustrophobic.'

'Get in.'

Happy pushed Wyatt's head down and shoved him hard. His thighs hit the lip of the boot. He fell forward, feeling Happy lift his legs and tumble him into the boot. Then the lid slammed behind him and he was in darkness again.

He lay there listening. The two men walked away from the car. He heard a steel door opening and a minute later he heard the uneven note of a diesel motor. It made a series of short snarls: Happy was backing it out of the panel-beating shed. Then the steel door crashed shut and footsteps approached the car. The car rocked a little as someone got in and shut the door. The engine started and they were moving.

The boot had been vacuumed recently. There was a faint pine perfume in the coarse fibres of the carpet under Wyatt. He began to search with his hands, running them into the corners.

Nothing. No tools, jack or wheel brace. He knew the spare tyre was in a recessed space under him but he took up most of the floor so he couldn't prise up the flap. He didn't think he'd find anything anyway. He tried the lock next. All he got out of that was grease on his fingers. And then the air around him began to shake and pound, lush and insistent. Jennifer Rush, 'The Power of Love.' That figured; that was the sort of cassette tape Trigg would own.

Wyatt reached up. The speakers were set in the wide shelf between the back seat and the big, sloping rear window. The shelf was made of some cheap, manufactured material. He could feel the vibrations in his fingers.

Wyatt approached the problem laterally. He couldn't get out of the car but he could go further in. He pushed upwards experimentally. He felt the shelf bend slightly. He waited through a pause between songs and explored the underside of the shelf until he found the holding screws. In time with the thudding bass he kicked at the area around the screws, stopping occasionally to test his progress. The shelf was tearing away from the screws.

When the shelf was moving freely he got into position. Stealth had got him this far. Now it was force all the way. The leads would tear away from the rear speakers but the front door speakers would continue to work. He waited while a song ended and another began. The opening bars were heavy and pounding. Wyatt heaved upwards, flipping the rear shelf down over the seat back, and dived through to the space behind Trigg.

The little man turned part-way around in shock, then tried to dig into his pocket with his free hand. 'Forget it,' Wyatt said, clamping his forearm around Trigg's neck. He reached down and retrieved the .38. The car swerved violently into the on-coming lane and back again. Wyatt increased the pressure on Trigg's larynx, released him, squeezed him again. 'Stop the car.'

Trigg steered off the road and pulled on the handbrake. Wyatt tickled the little man's ear with the .38. 'Turn that crap off.'

With the music gone the only sounds were the wind over the car and Trigg's frightened breathing. Trigg spoke first. 'We can work something out.'

Wyatt ducked his head and peered through the windscreen. There were red tail-lights in the darkness ahead of them. They went in and out of sight as the road dipped and turned between the black crops on either side.

Wyatt didn't want Happy to see that the headlights behind him were no longer moving. 'Turn the lights off.'

'Look, I can cut you in on some great action.'

'Turn the lights off.'

Trigg swung uselessly around at Wyatt. 'Do it,' Wyatt said. When the lights were off he said, 'Get out.'

Trigg had his door open a couple of seconds before Wyatt and he was twenty metres down the road, going hard, when Wyatt shot him. The bullet was like a punch in the back and Trigg sprawled face down on the road.

Wyatt picked up the body and put it in the front passenger seat. By now a minute had gone by and Happy would be wondering why instead of intermittent lights behind him there were none. Wyatt started the car and put his foot down.

He caught up with the truck a minute later and settled in close behind it. They travelled like that for ten minutes until he saw the truck's brake lights go on. Happy was turning into a lay-by. Wyatt followed in the car. A couple of road signs flared briefly in the headlights. Sharp curves ahead, they warned. Falling rocks.

Wyatt put the headlights on high beam and angled the car at the flank of the truck. He sat Trigg's body upright behind the steering wheel then stepped to the back of the car. He watched Happy get down from the truck cabin. The headlights were blinding the big man. He ducked his head as he approached the car and put his arm across his eyes. He was blinking, trying to get a response out of the little man who'd been his boss, when Wyatt shot him in the back of the head.

This was the final stage of a heist gone wrong but that didn't change the way that Wyatt went about it. He handled the steps one at a time, covering himself. He wiped his prints off the gun and tossed it away. He robbed the bodies and dragged them to the blind side of the truck and turned on the parking lights so no one would get too nosy. On his way back through Goyder he stopped to wipe his prints off Letterman's Valiant. Much later he passed within a few kilometres of Leah's house but he didn't think about her. He might later, when he'd got his money back from the Mesics and there were no more hired guns on his back.

This print edition published in collaboration with Brio Books,
an imprint of Booktopia Group Ltd

Level 6, 1A Homebush Bay Drive · Rhodes NSW 2138 · Australia

Print ISBN: 9781761281143

briobooks.com.au

MIX
Paper from
responsible sources
FSC® C008194
www.fsc.org

The paper in this book is FSC® certified.
FSC® promotes environmentally responsible,
socially beneficial and economically viable
management of the world's forests.